# Times Like These

a novel

# J. R. Klein

Publisher: Del Gato
Cover Image: Shalyapina
Library of Congress Control Number: 2022914306
ISBN: 978-1-7368101-7-0
ISBN: 978-1-7368101-8-7 (ebook)

Also by J. R. Klein

Frankie Jones
The Ostermann House
A Distant Past, An Uncertain Future
To Find: The Search for Meaning in Life on The
Gringo Trail
The Visitor
The Code
Quarter Rats
If I Could Do It All Again

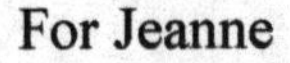

For Jeanne

"It was the best of times, it was the worst of times, it was the age of foolishness, it was the epoch of belief, it was the epoch of incredulity, it was the season of light, it was the season of darkness, it was the spring of hope, it was the winter of despair."

— Charles Dickens, *A Tale of Two Cities*

# PART 1

# 1

Owen Brookes and I were once particularly good friends. That was before the unfortunate incident between us, which I will get to in a minute.

I remember Owen as being strong and sturdy—something I always admired about him because it was very natural. It came from his father's side, I believe he once said. A kind of healthy, good physique that had not been honed in the gym. Owen detested that sort of thing—the artificially-muscular, exaggerated look—though I suspect in reality he detested it more from a sheer lack of desire on his part to spend hours with weights and pulleys and barbells than that he truthfully cared about how others allocated their time.

He was a handsome man though his natural insecurities left him with a sense of doubt when it came to women. And yet, women were uniformly drawn to him in a very spontaneous way. It is possible that he had once been married for a short period of time in his early twenties.

Owen came from a working-class family in Indianapolis and at one point his grandfather had made considerable money from mineral rights to a handful of oil wells that produced substantial revenue on a small piece of land south of the city. The rather sudden wealth had given the family a sort of celebrity status because it was during the height of the Depression when anyone with money was jealously revered.

The family moved into a large house where Owen's father grew up—a shiny black Packard sedan always out front. But, as the story goes, Owen's grandfather, being a terrible businessman, got himself snookered out of every nickel generated from the wells when he shared the mineral rights with a slick local lawyer.

Owen rarely talked about either of his parents except to say that he had been donated most of his good genes from his father, as I just alluded to. Beyond that, he said little and though I believe I remember hearing him once mention that he had a sister, and that both of his parents were still back in Indianapolis, and that except for the occasional trip to pay homage to some requisite holiday, Christmas or Thanksgiving or a birthday, he mostly despised the time spent there because it reminded him of all the failures life can cast upon us.

Owen was a photographer and a damn good one at that. He liked to brag that he had a camera in his hand from the time he was six. His first serious entry into photography began at the high school newspaper. However, it was when he won Best-of-Show for a photograph he entered in a state-wide contest that his chosen career path was sealed forever.

A week after graduating from high school he made his way to New York City in search of work. Little did he find and so he was relegated

to surviving off part-time jobs with various photography agencies and occasional work waiting
tables and once briefly as a doorman at a fine hotel on the upper East Side. It was there, greeting
the rich and the elegant of the city day in and day
out, that he got his big break when a senior editor
at *The New York Post* put in a word for him as a
junior staff photographer. Working for *The Post*
was the kind of thing Owen loved because, being
the raw tabloid that the paper was, it brought out
the dark side of Owen that always lurked just below the surface. He lasted at *The Post* barely two
years before joining the staff at the *San Diego
Sun*.

My name is Jack—Jack Carter. The details
of my life to this point are of little importance except to say I was abandoned as an infant by my
father, whom everyone called Big Hank, and was
orphaned at nine when my mother died. I grew
up in a school for boys in St. Louis until I was
sixteen. At nineteen I traveled the world and by
twenty-four I had put myself through college,

getting a degree in journalism. I earned my credentials as a junior scribe at the *Chicago Tribune* where I learned how the wheels of a big city newspaper turn and where I applied my natural intuitions and innate street sense as I pounded the boulevards and neighborhoods and back alleys of Chicago.

When a position came up at the *Boston Globe*, I grabbed it immediately. I loved living and working in Boston but within two years I found myself as a senior journalist with the *San Diego Sun*.

In truth, however, I never truly desired to be a journalist, my aspirations always had been to be a great writer of fiction. Indeed, all my life I had set my sites dubiously high. Odd, isn't it, that I would do that given the lousy cards I had been dealt as a child. But, after all, I had been down from the very start, so there was nowhere to go but up. I once read that there are only two tragedies in life: not getting what you want, and getting everything you want. How strange it is that success or failure in life is so heavily attributable to the cards we've been given. Strange.

Or how much is due to nature versus nurture, as is eternally argued by scholars and academics? In my case, it must have been nature, at least that's what I liked to believe. Consider that I knew very little personally about my mother, and even less about this person, Big Hank, yet I was endowed with a set of genes from both that formed my strong yet somewhat precarious psyche. So then, should we blame it on nurture? For me, a strange and mystifying form of nurture that was self-constructed from my days at the orphanage right up to the present.

I met Owen at *The Sun*. We were much alike. Working at the *Sun* was a time of great excitement and Owen and I became friends of the grandest kind, living in Del Mar and spending weekends at the beach or down in Baja—me, Owen, Anna, and Chloe. But it soured quickly after a moment of weakness between Anna and me. An unfortunate event that also tore apart the relationship between Owen and Anna and which indirectly ended up costing Owen his job at *The*

*Sun*.

I had not seen Owen for seven years. All I knew was that he had been hired by *Time* magazine and had promptly packed up and took off for somewhere in the Middle East. I confess, I had picked up an issue of *Time* fairly frequently during that time. And always inside was a prominent photo by Owen Brookes shot in the heat of some dire and dangerous situation. Whenever I saw one of Owen's photos, I found myself wondering why it was that some people whose path crosses ours stay with us in an absurd and persistent way. You cannot erase the memories of those people from your life. They are there to stay, indelibly seared deep into some neuronal recess forever. What is it about them that is so unique that they leave a residue of their own reality that becomes a part of us, part of our own marrow and gristle? I could not say, because they seemed little different from the droves of others I had encountered across years and decades.

As I sat many times looking at an Owen Brookes' photo, it was less the actual image being displayed, the one captured by the camera, than it was Owen, himself, that baited my wonderment. Each time I did this, each time my eyes locked onto an image, it resurrected memories of us in Del Mar or in La Jolla or in Tijuana or in Rosarito in Baja. And each time I found myself smiling, sometimes laughing brightly as we often did when we were together.

When Owen left, perhaps from boredom or perhaps from guilt, I am not sure which, I turned my attention to writing a novel. Having honed my skills with words during my years as a journalist, I thought I would be able to easily and adroitly adorn the pages of this book. Ah, how we fool ourselves! Writing good fiction is nothing like sowing words onto the pages of a newspaper. Three books I started and three books I rightly abandoned with frustrating sadness, not consigning so much as a single paragraph worthy of the page. To make matters worse, when I read back what I had written I realized I had committed all the sins, venial and mortal, that every new writer of fiction commits. It was a failure that threatened the very fiber of my existence. After all, wasn't I by profession a writer, wasn't it what I did every day to bring home a slice of bacon twice a month? Yes, how awfully well I had cheated myself with that deceitful assumption.

After a month of bathing my psyche in self-pity and burying every written page in the trash, and in the evenings sitting in Dini's on Sixth Street with a pint of stout or a sharp bolt of whiskey before me, I pursed my lips in determination and swore to try again.

In the mornings when I had an hour or two and on weekends when I had more time than that I took my laptop to the Del Mar Danish Pastry Shop and bought a sweet roll and a cup of coffee and tapped out the words of a novel under the eucalyptus trees in the courtyard behind the shop. It was not an easy slog and I had to fight to own each word. But when I was done, I had a story with big broad shoulders. A piece of fiction that detailed the lives of four people struggling to make a mark in a world where everything was changing fast. All chasing the beguiling and imponderable American Dream as I had done every second of my life.

I sent the manuscript off to an agent whom I knew. I was warned that the book was chancy, at best, but that she would give it a try with her most loyal editors. A few shot it down immediately, but one saw a deep and untapped theme that was missing in contemporary literary fiction. I signed a contract and they provided a paltry but welcomed advance of ten thousand dollars.

The book was published, rave reviews poured in. I was aghast and wondered in a disconcerting way if they had actually read the book I wrote. It quickly hit the *New York Times* best seller list and stayed there for months. Sales in the bookstores and on Amazon were robust. In the first year alone, I made almost four million dollars in royalties.

Vowing never again to work at *The Sun* or at any other newspaper I moved out of the converted garage apartment that had been my abode for many years and bought a sunny house on the west side of Camino Del Mar, close enough to the water to hear the ever-respiring ocean.

# 2

# 2

A soft Sunday breeze drifted in through the open living room windows as the doorbell rang. Standing before me was Owen Brookes. Seven years had changed him little. His jaw, still strong. His eyes, still deep and guarded. Owen's slightly large nose seemed more pronounced than I remembered and was possibly shifted ever so slightly to the left which, knowing Owen, might have been earned without consent given his vast and perpetual inkling for trouble. Yet, you could almost believe the change had improved his appearance, or certainly his inherent masculinity. His beard, once thick and full, was now short and speckled grey. And his head, which previously held a sweep of rich brown hair was shaved to the skin.

"Hello, Jack," Owen said lightly.

At a loss, all I could say was, "Owen," which came out more as a statement of surprise than a greeting.

"Well…am I going to stand out on the porch or are you going to invite me in?" Owen said with a small but convincing smile.

"Of course, yes, yes," I replied.

We walked through the house. Owen peered around with the quick eye of a photographer. He stopped and looked at an original Alfred Stieglitz photograph that hung in the living room: a horse-drawn taxi in New York in the middle of winter, steam rolling off the back of the horse.

We stood in the kitchen, both unsure of what to say.

"Well, I've got a month off," Owen said, leaning against the countertop. "I spent some time at home in Indiana and decided to make it over here to Del Mar. The *Sun* must be treating you well," he said, acknowledging the house.

"I left the *Sun* about the time my book came

out." My hand pulled open the refrigerator door and retrieved two bottles of Corona. We went to the back patio. The afternoon sun was angling toward the west, rendering a pale light onto the patio. Had Owen come to talk about what had happened seven years ago…I wondered?

Owen sat in a chair and took a long hit of beer and let the top of the bottle rest against his lower lip for a second—something I remembered him doing a thousand time. He took another hit and then set the bottle on the flagstones and slid back in the chair.

"Well, I guess first off I should say I know nothing came of the thing…you know, the thing between you and Anna. She got in touch with me barely two weeks after I left," Owen said.

I must have looked surprised.

"You didn't know, huh? She never told you?"

"We stopped seeing each other almost immediately."

Owen nodded with nonchalance.

"Anna's a damn good woman," I said.

"Damn good. Too good for the likes of me. Funny, but I've been haunted my whole life by kind and good women." A sudden feeling of ablution flushed through me as I membered the innumerable days Owen and I had talked about such things—how Big Hank, whom I never knew, had left me with a lingering flame of restlessness, an original sin I could not wipe from my soul.

"Aah…oh yes, she was a helluva fine woman, all right," Owen said. "But Anna and I would never have made it. How often did I say that even back then? Life's goals were different for us." He grunted and looked at the bottle of beer in his hand and said, "Well this much I know. We don't change very much, do we, Jack? No, not much. Instead of changing to life around us, we try to change the life we live in. Life moves faster and gets more complicated, but we stay the same desperate bastards we've always been."

The truth of Owen's words seemed to hang in the air.

"Do dreams come true, Jack? Remember how we used to wonder a lot about that? Well, I still think about it." Owen stopped speaking, then said, "I used to think life should be kind to us, and that it was only me who was getting screwed. I remember Anna once saying, 'Oh, for God's sake, Owen, it's not raining on you! It's just *raining*!'" He let out a loud and generous laugh, and then began to talk about his work with *Time*. He said he loved it, loved all of what he was doing and couldn't imagine doing anything else. "You know me, Jack, I always need to be where the action is." He pulled up his shirt and showed a scar on his right flank where a bullet had ripped through the flesh. "*Time* got me a two-thousand-millimeter lens and told me to get my ass out of the action. I was lucky. Yeah, the bullet missed all the important real estate. Burned like hell, though. Two days later I was out there again, patched up and working the camera like crazy."

"You always got too damn close to the action."

It was clear he liked it that way.

I got up and returned with two fresh bottles of beer.

"And a woman? What about that?" I said.

He studied the bottle of Corona for a second and gave a low sigh that was both happy and sad. With a look of sentience, he said, "Uh-huh…yeah. Rebecca…a Jewish girl I met in Beirut. God almighty! A real beauty…and hotter than hell's chimney. Gorgeous black eyes. Dark hair…wavy. She was a journalist." He pulled a snapshot from his wallet. They were in a café somewhere. Jerusalem, maybe, having drinks. Owen had his arm over her shoulder. They were looking at the camera, happy. I stared at the photo for quite a while and then handed it back to Owen, who placed it gently in his wallet.

He shook his head and said, "Ah…it never would have worked. I think I'm afraid of relationships, Jack. That's what I think. Christ, I've met the best women in the world, and I can't make it work to save my ass." He stared at the bottle in his hand as if contemplating what he had just imparted. His face betrayed truth and sadness. "So…so I read your book, Jack. It was good."

"It was a struggle."

"I got a copy at a kiosk along the Seine in Paris."

"They'll sell anything in those places."

"It was in a bookstore in Jerusalem, too, and even in Cairo."

"Did you recognize anyone…in the book?"

"Everyone. You, me, Anna, Chloe."

"Write about what you know. That's what they teach you."

Owen took a generous hit of beer and then said, "I knew you would write about our time."

"Did it bother you what I said about us? About you? About all of us?"

"It was true. How could I complain?"

"Sometimes the truth can be damn tough."

"Often it is," Owen replied.

"Yes, but fiction isn't truth, it's a facsimile of the truth. What you do is truth. Photographs are truth. They don't lie."

"Depends how they're used."

"Regrets about leaving the *Sun*?" I asked.

"Not for a second. I like my work in the Middle East. I hate flying in their damn planes, though. They go down a lot, a lot more than you hear about over here. And when I go to Africa or Russia, it's the worst of all. You never know if someone's planning to turn the whole damn plane into a huge Molotov cocktail."

"Sure, but getting into a car is infinitely more dangerous, and we do it every day," I said. "Riding down I-5 has become a near-death wish. All the goddamn nuts on the road going nowhere at eighty-five miles an hour. I'm thinking about getting out of here…maybe move to a place where I can live in peace and write."

"You're a lucky sonuvabitch. The luxury of being a writer, you can work wherever you want."

"If the energy to write is there," I replied. "Odd, though, I need a certain amount of personal interaction to write. I don't think I could write on a desert island even if I had everything I needed."

Owen leaned back. "See there…see, we're all victims of the world we live in. Kind of trapped, huh? Once when I was in Italy, I visited a monastery. It was way the hell up on a hill that looked down on a wonderful green valley. And inside the monks prayed and meditated in what seemed like perfect peace and harmony. And it was soothing and tranquil just being there. But I had a sort of crazy feeling that even there in the monastery, even in that sublime wholesome place, life was probably no different. Okay, sure, no one is planning to blow up a plane or run you off the road, but life can't be perfect…it never is. You know there is a monk who grinds his teeth, or something like that, when he says the rosary. And it pisses-off all the other monks. You *know* it happens."

Owen had arrived at the crux of a problem, a dilemma, I had struggled with for a long time. I had succeeded, or so it seemed, in gaining what I had long sought. I had written the book I thought would bring an inner peace to my soul. I had falsely equated success with contentment.

But all I had done was to expose myself to the world. Now when I went to La Jolla or to a restaurant in Del Mar or even when I walked down the street in Los Angeles or New York, people came up to me and told me how much they liked my book. And they shook my hand with esprit, as though I had cured them of some wretched undefined illness. Yet, I hadn't produced anything of mortal consequence, not really. I hadn't eliminated social injustice. I hadn't fed the world. I merely wrote a book.

"Tell you what, Jack, I'll be here a month. What say we go down to Mexico like we used to?"

"Jesus, that's a swell idea. Sure! Like we used to."

"Rosarito, San Felipe, Ensenada, Tijuana…Remember?" Owen leaned enthusiastically forward.

"Where are you staying?"

"At the Valencia Hotel in La Jolla…for now, at least. I could never afford such a thing when I was at the *Sun*. I used to wonder what it would be like. Now, I'm just like all the other pricks who stay at places like that." Owen shook his head and snickered. "Anyway, come down to La Jolla and we'll have a helluva time drinking margaritas at some saloon on Prospect Street, or at some hole in Pacific Beach like we used to. Remember? I've even thought of going to the *Sun* and seeing what's happening over there."

"Thought you promised never to set foot in the place again," I reminded him.

"Promises are easy to break. I'm good at it."

"I'm pretty damn good at it, too."

"Even thought of seeing Anna…you know, just to say hi."

"She's married. That's the last I heard. Living in a big place over in Rancho Santa Fe. She did the real estate stuff long enough to make a small fortune. I ran into Jeffrey Bickell from the *Sun*—he told me."

"Bunch of kids, I bet."

"Two, I think. She's married to a lawyer…some corporate greaser named Sam is what I heard. Together she and this Sam guy own about half of Fort Knox."

Owen nodded. "Well…she got what she always wanted. Anyway, isn't it interesting that we never think much about our past until we find ourselves right there where it happened." He glanced up at the vines that wove through the trestle above us. "It's been, what, seven years now since I was here. And, you know, I haven't thought about any of this crap for a rotten second and then all of a sudden now I'm wondering about it. I thought I had purged it from my soul long ago." Owen laughed weakly. "Ah, maybe I won't go see her after all," he added. "What's the point? Just digging up a lot of garbage from back then, huh? So, what's Chloe up to?"

"Chloe? She moved up to the Bay area shortly after you left. She stayed a while and then came back a year or so ago. She's become a helluva painter and sells her work at the good galleries around San Diego…Del Mar, La Jolla, Encinitas."

"Do you see each other?"

"Sure, all the time. She still looks great. You

know…that California look you see everywhere out here." I killed off my beer and set the bottle on the flagstone. "She has her own place up near Fifteenth Street but spends most of her time here. Turned her place into a studio."

"What about Mercedes?" Owen said quickly. "From when you were in Boston if I remember? You talked about here from time to time when we were at the *Sun*."

"Nah," I uttered. "Whole thing fell apart. Like with you and Anna. Anyway, time heals."

"If we let it, I suppose," Owen said.

"Whether we let it or not, I think."

"Okay."

For no reason I started talking about Big Hank. Owen knew quite a lot about him and how I had been forever haunted by a relentless and pithy urge to find a person I had never known.

"I keep imagining that someday I will run into Big Hank," I said, ruefully. "And yet I don't know what I would do if I found him. Would I be happy? Would I be mad? Would I be sad? Probably all of those…probably."

I told Owen about a recurrent dream I had had my whole life, even as a child. "I am in this room. It's dark and not a very attractive room, gloomy. I'm in bed and a man comes in and stands in the doorway and looks at me." I stopped speaking for a second. "I know this man is Big Hank even though I don't know what Big Hank looks like. He stands in the doorway and looks at me and says, 'I love you, Jack,' and then turns and leaves and shuts the door." I stopped talking and take a deep breath and let it out slowly. I looked at Owen. "Okay, we're getting pretty far down into the weeds," I said.

The sun toddled across the sky, bringing a wash of smooth vermillion that glowed lightly onto the patio. The green leaves of the lemon and orange trees took on a deep and shiny hue.

"Tell you what, Owen," I said. "How about we meet down in La Jolla for dinner?"

"At eight," Owen said, quickly grabbing onto the question.

"At eight."

"And Chloe, too."

# 3

After Owen left, I went to the sea and sat on a sandstone rock and watched the ocean for a while. The sun was all but gone, leaving a flash of pink and orange and red in its wake.

Though it was terrific to see Owen, it came with a torrent of memories. I was struck by how much he had kept alive his unremitting desire to peel away the tenebrous layers of life that trap us in a kind of foggy darkness, wittingly or unwittingly. As far back as I could remember I had searched for answers to questions that life guarded as though if it were to let them out, great cataclysmic consequences would beset the planet. And, who knows, perhaps that's exactly what might happen. How much of life should we be permitted to understand? Most of the animal kingdom operates in far more circumscribed niches. Yet we, humans, have evolved into a world of complexity, much of which we have become victims of by our own intelligence. Is an ever-sharper intellect a good thing? I wondered as I watched the ocean move repeatedly to the shore, only to turn away and try again.

The relentless activities of the ocean were for me a trigger, a neurotransmitter of sorts that could take me into a state of sheer bliss. A drug. On the mornings when I was unable to make a scintilla of progress on my book, I would come to the ocean and watch the waves as they arched sternly up and sank, finally moving timidly to shore in a thin layer that curtseyed on the rim of the sand. I would sit for hours, hypnotized by this. And out on the distance there always seemed to be a boat, a sailboat, spinnaker set to the sea perhaps in search of an island. Santa Catalina or San Clemente perhaps. I would return home filled with an inner vibrato that was just enough to push me through a few more troubled pages.

But now Owen's sudden and unexpected visit set within me a feeling of true joy. Even the ocean seemed less fearsome. I always had a mistrust for the power of Nature. Not because I felt that Nature was evil or destructive—though sometimes it can appear to be—but it was rather a fear that came from not being able to hold its power in check. How silly! Me, all of us collectively, being able to control a powerful force of Nature. When I traveled the world as a young man many years ago, I saw how Nature can take and destroy what we, we humans, had strapped together in the flimsiest sort of way in an effort to protects ourselves from the world around us.

There are some people among us who have a kind of strength, a swagger you might say, that the rest of us lack, that the rest of us will never quite have. We all know these people. Well, Owen for sure had it. He had it back when he was living in Del Mar working at the *Sun*. A kind of bravado that irritated the other photographers at the newspaper. I watched, sometimes with glee as they seethed in his presence. And yet, Owen never boasted an attitude of superiority other than to let it emerge freely when he was in the presence of others. For me, I found it refreshing that a kid from the Midwest who bore a set of genes he largely detested was a source of irritation to so many who forever crowed about their skills and achievements.

Yes, Owen was right when he declared we don't change very much. When you come right down to it, personal adaptation is not a strong suit for our species. We are all far more obsessive, far more neurotic, far more eager, far more aggressive, than we like to believe. Well, I for sure am. Of that, I am certain. For that matter, entire societies bear the burden of obsessiveness. This I saw when I traveled the world as a young man and witnessed how people continually led themselves haphazardly into a sconce of self-destruction.

Before I knew it, the last desperate rays of sunlight had curled below the horizon. I got up and returned home.

✱

Owen was at the bar when Chloe and I

arrived at a Mexican restaurant called Guerrero's—one of many similar upscale spots in La Jolla and throughout San Diego. Owen immediately flagged the bartender. When our drinks arrived, we toasted to Owen's return to Southern California.

"Christ almighty, I haven't had an enchilada or a taco or a tamale in years," Owen uttered almost painfully.

"Well, you won't be disappointed," Chloe said.

"Funny how much some places stay the same and other places perpetually change," Owen declared. "La Jolla never changes much…does it?" His eyes studied the room. He turned to the windows behind us that opened onto Prospect Street where people sauntered past in smart summer clothes. "Well, I don't know, maybe it's a good thing. You know I never liked the way America is always fussing and changing everything. I never figured that out." He took a sip of his margarita and licked the salt from his lips.

A woman came by and said, "Excuse me, I don't mean to interrupt, but are you the author Jack Carter?"

I nodded.

"I read your book. I loved it," she said. "I told all my friends about it."

I thanked her.

After she left, Owen said, "Well, I see you've become quite the celebrity."

"My fifteen minutes of fame."

"Well, enjoy it while you can, I always tell him," Chloe said.

"I'm not sure how much I enjoy it."

"He does…he does. Jack is very good at pretending to be annoyed," Chloe said.

"I think I remember," Owen said. "See how little we change."

"And I still like salty margaritas, too," I replied with a smirk. "Yes, I have changed very little since you were here in Del Mar," I told Owen.

The hostess led us to a table. A waiter set down a bowl of chips and salsa. Owen ordered a round of margaritas.

We paged through the menu. When the waiter brought the drinks, we ordered dinner. Owen had chicken enchiladas with mole. Chloe and I had tacos. Owen ate like he had just come off a hunger strike.

A woman we knew from our time at the *Sun* came up to the table. She worked in circulation; her name was Jolene. I remembered her quite well. She was fun and easy going. All the time we worked at the *Sun* she had a thing for Owen. It was evident to everyone. Everyone but to Owen who at that time tried hard to stay faithful to Anna.

"Well, my, my, I believe this is Owen Brooks that I see here." A spark of enthusiasm lit her voice.

"In the flesh, my dear," Owen replied.

"And where have you been, my darling young one?" Jolene said, tagging a line from Bob Dylan's song.

"Just about everywhere, honey…just about everywhere."

"That's what I heard. Have you returned to

stay?"

"Nope…only a short visit, Owen replied with a rather sorrowful smile. "A few weeks, that's all."

"Well…tell you what. There's a party tonight over at Oscar's. Remember Oscar? He throws great parties. He's a journalist like Jack here used to be. Before he became rich and famous."

"Before he became tired and boring," I retorted.

"So, come to Oscar's when you're done. It's just down the street around the corner. Remember?"

I nodded.

"The whole gang will be there. *Ciao!*" she said. She looked at Owen and gave a wink and was off.

"What do you think," Owen posed. "Should we go?"

"Up to you, old boy," I said.

"Why pass up a free party?" Chloe said.

"Who do you think will be there? That

bastard Bradford Brice?"

"Probably," I replied.

Owen growled.

"Avoid him. The others are fine," I said.

"How do you avoid someone like Bradford Brice?"

"You can," I said.

"He's a disease…worse than smallpox."

"Then pretend your vaccinated," Chloe said.

"Anyway, it might be fun to see the others. Don't you think?" I said.

"Do you keep in touch with them?"

"No, not much," I replied.

"Okay, see there, Jack. Why keep in touch with that bunch of dimwits?" Owen posed.

"Uh, I'm too busy, that's all. When I worked at the *Sun*, I had lots of time. Remember how it was? Now I *should* have lots of time and I have none. I'm trapped in my own curse. I got what I wanted but sometimes I wonder what the hell I really got."

"I told you, Jack loves to complain," Chloe said. "He's very good at it."

"And I still love you," I said to Chloe, and gave her a kiss.

"A dream that came true…is that it? You got what you wanted and now it's killing you," Owen murmured.

I laughed and shrugged.

"Okay now, we'll all go to Oscar's after this. Why not?" Owen said. "There are a few from the *Sun* I wouldn't mind seeing again."

"Sure, you don't owe them anything. Neither do I. We went our own way and I think it's been good for us. Tough at times, but good," I said.

"And if that bastard Brice, as you say, is there, we leave," Chloe said.

"That will be hard to do without knocking him on his ass first, just for old time's sake."

"Self-control," old boy. "Self-control," I said.

Owen had a third margarita. The expression on his face, his ever-watchful darting eyes, had become less cautious. I sensed that the years at the magazine had worn heavily on his usually tight-strung nerves. That was Owen. Someone who saw, someone who witnessed, who experienced—even if only visually—everything that was happening around him. Some people watch the world, some people experience it. Others are never part of it no matter how deeply it penetrates into their lives.

"While we're at it, tell me what you think. Do you think I should go see Anna while I'm here?" Owen asked Chloe. "Jack and I decided it's probably all right. You know, she's married and has kids and all, and is probably happy as hell…who knows? So—"

"I had an experience like that once when an old flame showed up at the door," Chloe said. "It was quite awkward."

Owen thought it out for a second. "Yeah. And anyway, even if she never got married, it wouldn't have worked between us. We were oil and water." He laughed gratuitously. "But here's the rub. I was never able to clearly wipe Anna from my thoughts after I left. Crazy as it seems, I thought about her a lot while I was gone. I sort of fabricated a world, an alternate universe in which we were perfectly matched…Anna and me. Like two perfect Zodiacs where everything fits in true harmony. Ha, ha! And then I almost believed that things between us could have worked out. Yeah, I almost believed it. I think our psyche plays some awful tricks on us at times. It wants us to believe the impossible."

I explained again that Big Hank was the only person in my life whom I could never forget, whose memory I carried with me each and every day, though in truth I remember practically nothing about him. And I explained how I often wished I could move beyond that part of my dark and submerged memory. Yes, Owen was right, our psyche taunts us with many memories whether we like them or not.

Owen said, "I even used to think Anna would like it the Middle East, and that she would enjoy the good places, the ones that were pleasant. Israel, for example, which I especially liked. And Istanbul and Cairo, too. The bazaar at Khan Al-Khalili. It's a world unto itself."

4

Walking into Oscar's, feeling woozy from the margaritas, I was hit with a thunder of music playing from a CD player. The room was a crop of people, some of whom I recognized, some of whom I didn't.

It wasn't long before Oscar came beaming up to us like we were great celebrities who showed up unexpectedly at his party. He had changed little in the almost five years since I had left the *Sun*. Warm smile, dark Hispanic eyes. He shook our hands with great vigor and explained what a surprise it was to see us, and led us to a kitchen counter that was teeming with beverages of all sorts. I couldn't handle another margarita, so I pulled a Modelo from the ice chest. Owen and Chloe did likewise.

Jolene jostled up to us through a room constricted with people. "*Well* what do you know, you came," she said, as if she expected a no-show.

"Your invitation was too alluring," Owen replied.

Jolene laughed a tipsy laugh. "Or maybe you had nothing better to do…perhaps that?"

"Or too much to do and this was a good way not to do it," Owen laughed.

"I'm so glad you're back in San Diego, Owen. I do wish you'd stay. I really do. See what it's like here. We always had fun, all of us from the *Sun*. Remember…huh?"

Owen nodded. His face suggested he remembered the good moments of that time very well.

"Okay, Owen," Jolene said, grabbing him by the arm, "come on, let's dance!"

Owen set his beer on the counter and followed Jolene into the room where a legion of people gyrated in all forms of human motion.

Standing there watching the hustle-bustle of the room, the alcohol wore fast on my thoughts. I recalled my time at the *Sun*, and yes, thought about Mercedes even. I was right when I told Owen I hadn't thought of her in quite a few years. Or at least that's what I mostly liked to believe. But, yes, Owen was right when he spoke of those people who pass through our life and leave a long and permanent mark on it, like the tail of a comet after it has passed across the sky. And yet, oddly, I really had little interest in seeing Mercedes again. I had conflated those two possibilities: seeing her and putting the thought of her away forever, so that at times one version won out, at other times the other version won.

Jarring music filled the room.

"Wanna dance?" Chloe said, swinging to the sound.

"Sure, in a second."

I found myself queerly content to be with the group from the *Sun* that I thought I had left behind forever. How is it that when we leave something and then revisit it, we are often delivered a completely different version from the one we think we remembered? Looking around, feeling the energy in the room, I had a sense of comfort that I occasionally experienced during my days at the *Sun*. A sense of confidence in what I was doing at that time.

I felt a tap on my shoulder. "Jack Carter?"

I turned to find one of my editors from the *Sun*.

"I was told you left San Diego," he said. "That's what I heard."

"Rumors grow from nowhere," I replied. "Leave Camelot…nah."

His name was Dexter Morris. A likeable fellow with a sharp carved face who always bore the look of some sixteenth century potentate. We got along very well. He often pushed my work to the front page even when it didn't deserve it. I was never too sure why, but never questioned it and was happy he did. It's always easy to rationalize a good turn of events when it has to do with oneself whether we deserve it or not.

I introduced Chloe.

"Sure, I remember from when Jack was at the *Sun*."

We talked about the *Sun*. Dexter always struck me as the kind of person who would be doing at sixty exactly what he had been doing at forty. That rare person who had hooked his dream early in life and would never leave it. That's what I saw in Dexter Morris—a sensible man with godly patience when it came to working with people, especially the mercurial cub reporters who demanded bold assignments. I knew all about it. I had started out that way in Chicago and Boston, forever pushing editors for jobs that were well beyond my paygrade.

"The paper is doing okay," Dexter Morris said. "You know…same old crap. Cute stories about day care centers in Escondido, or zoning in Ocean Beach. Shit like that…the earth-shaking stuff." He laughed impulsively. "The earth-shaking stuff," he repeated. "The crap *The New York Times* won't go near because it's too explosive." He laughed again, this time so hard his shoulders rocked.

He explained that he had been offered several jobs at good papers and had passed on all of them. All were in cities up in the "frozen north" as he put it.

"But, of course, when I came to San Diego a while back it was a different place than today," Dexter said. "Now, it's growing like a tumor—a big, fat, metastatic tumor! The city needs to do something about it. Do you know how many articles we've written about that?"

"I remember writing a few myself," I told him.

Dexter nodded. "Of course, there's nothing the city can really do. Not really. You can't stop people from coming here," he said, looking grim and turning away. "Ugh! Well, anyway, it won't be long before papers like the *Sun* go belly-up, so it doesn't really matter to me. Nobody reads newspapers these days but the old farts who can't work a computer. You got out just in time, Jack. I mean it. I've been trying to think of what I'll do when the damn thing finally collapses."

We had migrated over to where the drinks

were. Dexter pulled a beer from the cooler.

"The on-line stuff is doing well, though," Dexter said. "I don't mean the garbage crap. I mean the good stuff like Huff Post…that stuff. I could always work for something like that, I suppose.

"Sure, and you can do it from anywhere. You can do it from your house. No need to pack up for the frozen north.

"I read your book. I liked it…even the stuff about the *Sun*."

"Write about what you know," I repeated yet again. "That's what they tell you in school."

"Christ, the book's in every store in La Jolla and Del Mar, all the bookstores, big and small ones, even the supermarkets."

"Uh-huh…it's done well."

"I've been considering a book," Dexter said.

"You should."

He shrugged slightly. "Fiction is not in the cards. That I can tell you. Maybe a biography. Yeah…a biography maybe."

"The biography market is big," I said.

"I was always able to write fast when I was a reporter. But that's crud you do for newspapers. You know, the junk people use to line their parakeet cage with when they're done reading it. I want something I can dig my teeth into, something I can research."

Owen and Jolene returned. They were energized by the music. Laughing, Jolene said, "Owen is great. I'm blasted. Wow!" She kissed him on the cheek. They grabbed a drink from the table.

Owen wiped perspiration from his brow. "Come on," he told Jolene. "Let's get some air on the balcony."

"Well anyway, I'm giving the biography thing serious thought," Dexter said. "I'll have to pick the right person, though. No damn politicians, that's for damn sure. We write about them too much at the paper. All the rags do—you know that. And besides, most of them, the pols, bore the be-jesus out of me. Nothing but a bunch of self-centered little bastards…huh! A scientist, I'm thinking about that. They're more decent than politicians at least…and more truthful, I think."

My eyes were drawn to the corner of the room just as Anna, Owen's old flame from our time together, walked in. I was shocked to see her. This ought to be lovely, I thought…wait until Owen comes in from the balcony. Even Dexter Morris, who only knew Anna from a few events that she had come to with Owen, sensed the situation it might create. He looked at me.

"Do you know Anna?" I asked.

"We met a couple of times when Owen worked at the *Sun*."

"They split up and she got married pretty quick," I explained. "Here she is…hold your hat."

Moments later, Owen and Jolene returned from the balcony. It didn't take long before his eyes landed on Anna. I could all but hear his heart jump. Both stood stone-cold motionless. Anna worked her way across the room. Speechless at first, she said, "My God, Owen, where the hell did you come from?"

"Well, that seems to be the question of the hour," he replied.

It helped to break the ice.

"How are you doing?"

A nod and a smile that withered rather quickly. "Jack says you got a place up in Rancho Santa Fe."

"Yes, a quaint little flat," she said, looking away.

We all knew there were no quaint little flats in Ranch Santa Fe.

I could tell Owen was bursting to find out why Sam was not with Anna. But even Owen, known for his singular ability to insert his foot squarely in his mouth, managed to adroitly steer shy of the issue.

Chloe pulled me onto the dance floor, a move which drew no resistance from me. Later in the evening the five of us gathered, laughing, talking, having fun. To the benefit of all, Bradford Brice, Owen's arch nemesis from his days at the paper, did not make an appearance that night.

5

I did not see Owen again for two days. I tried working on my book but had little success. One flimsy chapter. A few flimsy paragraphs that had to be scrapped to protect my self-esteem.

I was heading down to the low cliffs that looked onto the ocean from above Thirteenth Street when my cell phone rang. It was barely nine a.m.

"Jack. We're going down to Rosarito, just like we used to. Remember?"

"Who?"

"Me and Anna. Like we used to. Remember? Come on along. We'll have a helluva good time."

The thought occurred to me that this was

one of Owen's weird jokes. He was known to throw one out now and then. I enquired if it was.

"No, absolutely not. It was Anna's idea. She wants to go. Remember how we all used to do it? The four of us? You, me Anna, Chloe? What do you say?"

I didn't think hard about it. "When?"

"An hour. Get Chloe, too."

"She's going over to a gallery today. I doubt she can make it. I'll check."

"Yes, do. Anyway, we'll pick you up. And bring a swimsuit."

When they came by, Owen was sitting in the driver seat of an expensive Land Rover. I climbed in the back.

"It's Anna's car," Owen said right off.

"Yes, this is what being married to a rich lawyer gets you. This and a silver Maserati."

"Handles like a Learjet," Owen said.

We headed south on I-5. The day was clear and bright and blessed with warm soft air. We arrived at the border where cars were backed up for several blocks but moved quickly across. In twenty minutes, we were in Tijuana on Hwy 1. Owen aimed the car west and picked up Hwy 1D that skirts along the coast of Baja.

Immediately, the air was filled with the smell of dry dirt, that ever-present reminder that we were in Mexico. I often thought that if I were blindfolded and placed magically down in Mexico, I would recognize it instantly. Fragrances that grew up from the arid earth below us, the balm of fresh food that hailed from the adobe houses as we passed through small towns. Off to our right, an endless spread of blue Pacific lay motionless until it churned and bubbled onto the shore. Sea mist that you could almost taste filled the air.

My curiosity about why Anna wanted to go to Rosarito was sharp. What had happened to her marriage, I wondered? But I knew in time I would find out today. If anything could be said about the time the four of us had spent together years ago, it was that sooner or later all the laundry—dirty and clean—would come out. Dumped in one big pile on the floor.

"It will be wonderful to sit on the veranda at Rosarito and watch the ocean," Owen said. "Have some tacos, maybe. Have a cold drink…a beer, margaritas. Funny, but when I was working half-way around the world, I would find myself thinking about Rosarito and the great time we spent there."

Owen swerved sharply to avoid a cluster of potholes. "Love that Mexican technology," he uttered.

"Well, I haven't been to Rosarito since we all came down here together, when was it?" I asked. "Seems like an awfully long time ago. Doesn't it."

We cut through the town of Santa Teresita—humble and simple—and continued past Santa Monica Sur until we reached Playas de Rosarito, passing adobe buildings and houses and palm-lined boulevards. High above us on the hill was the statue of El Christo de Rosarito—arms outstretched and looming heavily over the village and the far-off sea.

Owen parked the car in the hotel lot. We

gathered our bags and walked through the lobby. Everything was exactly as I remembered it. The rotunda. The elaborately decorated Mexican tiles. Guests sat leisurely on leather-padded dark wooden chairs and sofas drinking and eating. Waiters carried trays banked high overhead with platters of food of all kinds. This was Mexico and Mexico does not change, the world merely evolves around it and Mexico assumes some of it, as much as it wants, but not a bit more.

On the veranda we located a table with a striped umbrella that shaded us from the simmering sun as it slow-crawled across the sky. Owen ordered a pitcher of margaritas. It seemed like the right choice for our unplanned reunion.

When the pitcher arrived, the waiter poured a glass for each of us. No sooner had Owen taken a sip than he opened up. Speaking in a very round and philosophical voice, he said, "You know, I've been thinking. I'm wondering if maybe I should wrap things up with *Time* and see what other work is out there. It's certainly been a good experience, at *Time* I mean, and I don't regret a minute of it."

"I think you should, Owen," Anna said, quite eagerly. "Well, now what I mean is, you should do what you want to do, of course. You could always come back and work in San Diego, don't you think?"

Owen leaned back and puffed out his cheeks and nodded several times rather thoughtfully. It was obvious this was not the first time the idea had passed his mind.

"You don't have to work at the *Sun*, of course," Anna continued. "I know you hated it there."

Owen rolled his eyes and took a generous sip of the salty cocktail and set the glass on the table, then breathed deeply.

"Good photographers are always in demand in San Diego," I said.

"Well, anyway, what I know is that America is getting more hostile all the time," Owen said, "I can tell you from what I learned with the magazine that hatred breeds hatred. You wonder where it will end. Walk down any street in any city in the States and the first thing you notice is how different we all are. It should be a strength for us. Afterall, we're nothing but a rag-tag bunch of immigrants no matter how long ago our ancestors arrived here. Yesterday or four-hundred years ago…it doesn't fucking matter where you're from. If you're not a Native American, you're just a newbie. Period! Some people think they have a right to be here and others don't. And you know what really pisses me off? People think that you get ahead by keeping others down. Let me tell you, I saw a hell of a lot of that when I was on assignment in crappy little third-world countries. The problem is that in the poor countries, there isn't enough pie to go around, so…"

"But that's not true here, is it?" Anna said abruptly.

"Hell no," Owen retorted. "There's plenty of pie. More than enough. You really don't realize it until you see what it's like elsewhere." He folded his arms, leaned toward the table, and said, "The real damn problem with the planet is that we're breeding ourselves right out of existence. What is it now, eight billion people, something like that, and more on the way?"

A woman in the skimpiest string bikini passed the table on her way to the water. I tried not to stare.

Owen said, "You know, there's a part of me that wants to do what you said, Jack. Find a place where there's no one to bug you. Let the whole goddamn world go to hell. Sure, I like what I'm doing," he said with a tone of uncertainty. "But let me tell you, it gets tough, day in, day out heading to some rotten village or town or spot on the globe. You see a lot of shit you wished you hadn't. And yet, that's what I'm there for. To see it, to record it. Get a load of that. Well, it can wear you down. Some of the people who've been at it for a long time at the magazine seem to be immune to it. And yet I know that's not true. When you talk to them, you find out that all the crap we deal with every day, well, they just keep it inside more. I guess I'm not quite there yet. Maybe never will be…who knows?" He shrugged as if to accept his fate.

"There is something terribly restless about Americans," I said. "It's something I keep coming back to in my books. I think that's why the first one did well. Americans related to it. Americans are never truly happy. We always want more. We believe it's our birthright, and it makes us restless as hell. Those bastards who came here from some dump in Europe or wherever believed they were breaking free from the poverty that had stricken their families forever. But then reality delivered a hefty punch the second they climbed out of steerage and set foot in America. They found themselves in sweatshops in New York working fourteen hours a day. Or in coal mines in Appalachia. Or scratching out a living in the red dirt of Oklahoma like Tom Joad did in *The Grapes of Wrath*. So, what do they do? They set out on another odyssey to get away from the first one. It's an odyssey of escape…what we Americans do, what we have always done. Despite what we might think we are not on an odyssey of discovery. No. Not a bit. We are on an odyssey of escape."

"You really believe that?" Owen dubiously said.

"Quite."

Owen gave his drink a swirl.

"You might not think it, but most of the time it doesn't matter whether our dreams come true or not. Most of the time we have little control over our fate," I said. "What matters is that we keep dreaming. That's what I figured out. It's the dream that matters."

"Well, we all want our dreams to come true. Don't you, Jack?" Anna said.

"Sure. Of course, I do."

"And if they don't?"

"What can I do? Hope for more, that's all."

"Is the American Dream a hoax, then?" Owen plied.

"Maybe…I'm not sure. Is it real?" I asked.

"It can be, I think," Owen said. "The world wants to dream like Americans do, that much I know. The reason is simple—most people have no chance to make their dreams come true. They are victimized by the circumstances of their lives."

"Well, the way I see it is that it's not the dream that matters, it's the hope of the dream that matters."

"I don't know, that sounds terribly futile," Anna said.

"No, I think there *is* a difference. You can take away someone's dream, but you can't take away their hope. Dreams have to be lived, but hope is inside us."

Anna groaned softly. "Well, I hate to say it, but you might be right, Jack. I never quite thought of it like that. I believed I was happy when I was married. And I was…for a while, I guess. At least that's what I thought. And my kids are great, of course. So, I'm happy of that. But what do you do when you know the rest of your life is not right? That it just flat-out sucks? How long do you wait? That's what I kept wondering. You wait and hope it will get better and one day you realize it won't. This is the way it is and the way it's going to stay. It's a grim thought. And it doesn't matter how much money you have because even here in America, even in glorious Rancho Santa Fe, hope can be as fickle as the sea breeze. Now here…now gone."

"Yes, I've been thinking about that for a long, long time," Owen said. "I'm still wondering about it, I guess."

"Well, this much I know. We change what we can and put up with the rest," I said. "Life can deal an awfully bad hand at times. The day comes when we need to let some of the cards go and pick up a few new ones and hope for the best."

"And then you find that the new cards are no better. Then what?" Owen said. "Then what?"

Anna winced. "Yes, that's the real risk, I think. Getting a worse hand than what you started with." She looked silently out at the lawn of sand and the clear blue water that lay on the horizon. "Well, finally dumping Sam was a good thing for me. I found out he had been screwing around for a long time. And, stupid me, I didn't know a thing about it."

Owen listened carefully as if hoping to get all the harsh details.

A waiter set a bowl of tortilla chips and salsa on the table and refilled the margarita glasses.

"As soon as I learned about it, the decision to leave was easy," Anna said. "I got in touch with Frank Berman…remember Frank?"

We both shook our head.

"Oh…he did some work for me back in the days I was peddling houses," Anna said. "When I filed for divorce, I knew I needed a good lawyer because Sam would come at me with both barrels loaded and try to get at me for filing for divorce. And he tried. Damn right he tried. He tried to screw me out of every damn penny we had. It was damn nasty, the divorce, but in the end, I got my fair share. That's all I wanted. I got the house in Rancho Santa Fe, some money, and the kids. He got some cash, some stocks, our house in the Caribbean, and the boat. Fine take the damn boat and sail away with that little slut of yours. That's how I felt about it."

Listening to Anna, I sensed that she had been through a lot. I knew from my own experiences how all the bad crap that happens to us in life can leave permanent scars and welts on our psyche that never fully heal. And yet despite it all I saw a lustrous sparkle in Anna's eyes. If I remembered one thing about her, it was that her deep and refulgent eyes seemed to hold all the secrets of her life. A kind of glow that some people own and carry with them. Eyes that spoke of happiness and joy no matter what.

"So now what?" Owen asked.

"Oh, you know. Be a good mom. Maybe someday go back to peddling houses again…maybe. You know, just to keep myself busy. Who knows? But I'd kind of like to get out of Rancho Santa Fe. It was really Sam's idea, not mine. In fact, I never liked it. Too snooty and stuffy for me. Everything's too perfect…Stepford Wives."

"There's always Del Mar again," I said. "Or La Jolla."

Anna's brow arched up. "Oh yeah…I've considered it. I still have good memories of our time there along the coast. We had fun."

"Ah, fun we did have," Owen agreed,

broadly smiling.

"You know what I'm considering, though?" Anna said. "Somewhere here in Mexico, perhaps. But I need a place where the schools are good for the kids. Life in the States is getting much too tedious. Faster and more complicated all the time. I'd like to find a place where everything is slower."

"Greece appeals to me," Owen said, "So does Italy. There is a great little town in Italy down in the boot called Matera. I fell in love with it the first time I was there. The climate is nice. Almost like in Central Mexico."

"San Felipe, too. Over on the gulf side of Baja. Oh yeah, we had a lot of fun over there, didn't we?" I said.

The smell of food swirled around us. It was approaching one o'clock. Owen said, "Come on, let's order something." He flagged the waiter who brought menus. "Well, it's *huachinango* for me...I don't need the menu. And a cold bottle of beer. What's more Mexican than that?"

Anna and I followed suit. In no time the

waiter brought three platers of fried *huach-inango*—red snapper with sliced cabbage and onion and tomato and avocado, and crispy French fries. Three bottles of Cerveza Pacifico and iced glasses were set down.

"And when we're done, we'll go for a swim in the ocean. What do you think?" Owen said. "The water looks wonderful."

"Here, I've got an idea. What do you think about this?" Anna said. "Why don't we see if they have rooms at the hotel. We could each get one and spend the night in Rosarito. I can get in touch with my housekeeper. I know she'll be willing to take care of the kids. What do you think?"

"That's a swell idea," I said. "It would be a shame to come down here and not enjoy the whole day. It's a grand idea. Okay, after we eat, I'll check about rooms."

The *huachinango* was glorious. Nothing better in all of Mexico. When we finished lunch, I went to the desk clerk and secured three rooms.

"We're in luck," I said when I returned. "A

room for each of us."

We changed into our swimsuits. A half hour and we were standing on the edge of the water. The tide was low and the waves were breaking in foamy rolling crests.

I couldn't help catching a glimpse of Anna. Firm and svelte in a black suit that was cut high on her hips. No matter what life had dished out to her in the past few years, she seemed to have fared well during her time in Rancho Santa Fe.

We stood on the edge of the water watching the breakers work their way piously onto the shore one after another from the deep aqua water far out where the sea melded with the sky.

Owen waded out. He stood up to his knees in the water and turned and said, "Get ready…it's damn cold." He charged in and dove through a wave and came up and yelled, "Okay, you chicken asses. Get in here!"

I looked at Anna. "All right, then…let's go."

Anna cringed.

"All together," I said.

"You go. I'll watch," Anna said.

"It'll be good once you get used to it."

"The only thing I'm used to is my warm pool in Rancho Santa Fe," she declared.

"Then, this will be good. For both of us."

"For you. I have given up pain for Lent."

"But it is not Lent yet."

"Then I am practicing so I can be ready when Lent comes. When is it, anyway?"

"I don't know. I gave up Lent."

We waded a short distance into the water together and stood motionless as Owen had done. He was right when he said it was cold. Owen had now moved beyond the breakers and was bobbing like a gull in the undulating sea.

"Come on," he yelled. "Once you're in, it's perfect."

I glanced at the sky. The sun was straight up and glaring down with a Cyclopean eye that filled the seaside in harsh whiteness.

"If I go, will you?" I asked Anna.

"Well, of course," she replied in the most unconvincing way.

"Yes, of course, and did I ever tell you I

once swam from Del Mar to Japan…and back again."

Anna laughed, toying coyly with my belief that she would follow if I led.

"And so now we will both go," I said. "Ah…see, see how the water has warmed already while we stood here."

"You have a grand imagination," Anna claimed. "No wonder you're a writer of fiction."

Owen called to us again.

"Okay, here goes," I said. I rushed into the water and dove forward and came up and looked at Anna. I knew she would eventually make her way in. She reached down and splashed water across her face and onto her hair. "If I freeze, it's your fault," she yelled and dove in.

Owen swam to where Anna and I were standing. The water had to be given respect because of its tricky and wily currents and unpredictable riptides.

"If you go out just a little more you can catch a wave and ride it in," Owen said, "It's a helluva lot of fun."

We followed Owen. He said, "There will be a good wave coming in a sec. Just wait."

Soon, one billowed up and was moving quickly toward us.

"Okay, here it is. Just before it hits swim like a sonuvabitch and let it grab you."

The wave raised us in perfect unison like small plastic toys and carried us to the beach. We did this again and again until even Owen was numbed by the chill of the water. We lumbered across the beach and spread our towels on the sand and flopped down and toasted in the sun that was creeping slowly westward.

Anna brushed hair across her head. She had a pure and natural beauty that was more stunning than I remembered from our previous time to-gether. It made me wonder why it was that some people—women and men both—seem to get bet-ter looking as time passes, seem to defy the natu-ral laws of time and aging. The laws of gravity. There was always something about Anna, and I can't tell you what it was, that made her stand out from the rest of us. If you saw her on the street,

you might turn and look, believing she was someone you had seen in a magazine perhaps. Maybe
mistake her for some vaguely familiar famous
person.

"I feel tremendous," Owen said. "There is
something about the sea. It has so much power
and energy. I feel as though it gives some of it to
me when I'm in the water."

"It was a great idea to come here," I said.

"Anna suggested it," Owen replied.

"I guess I needed to get away if only for a
day. I'm stuck in my life right now," Anna said.

Owen sat cross-legged. He seemed to be
thinking about what Anna had just said, as if contemplating some recondite dilemma. He reached
over and picked up a small handful of sand and
let it trickle through his fingers again and again.
He spoke, saying, "Well, it's times like these that
make us feel that way. That's how I see it." He
looked at me. "You know what I mean, don't
you?"

I shook my head.

"Times like these," Owen repeated. "You

know, like we said before about how the world is all screwed up and it's not getting better. And it makes us want to get away from it, doesn't it? To run and hide like a child."

"Here's what bothers me most," Anna said quickly. "You're right. The world is more screwed up than ever. I think about that almost all the time now because I have two small children. Sure, I can take care of them. And sure, I probably always will be able to…while they're young at least. But look, they are barely five-years old. Do you know that the life expectancy is now approaching a hundred years in this country? Think of that. What will the world be like for them in a hundred years? In the year 2100, let's say? How many people ever stop to think about that before they have children? Well, I know I didn't."

Owen nodded. "And to top it off, the world is getting meaner and more uncivil by the minute. Like I said before, when you do what I do and every couple of days you're off to another screwed up part of the world it's hard to see how it will ever get better. Just look at how it is here in the States. The country is becoming so filled with anger."

"It worries me," Anna said, running the brush through her hair. You try to raise kids and hope it won't affect them. And it's the complexity of life that I worry about, too. Can anyone keep up with it? Computers…technology. Look what it's done to us."

Owen said, "It won't be long until personal privacy will be archaic. Like those dinosaur bones they dig up in North Dakota or wherever. Believe me, the day is coming. But nobody thinks much about it. George Orwell, he had it pegged perfectly."

"1984…Winston Smith. Every moment, every movement monitored," I said. "Yeah, I know this sounds like a bunch of conspiracy shit. I know it does. But if you own a computer, not one bit of your life is safe."

"So where do we go from here, the four of us? You guys and me and Chloe…to get away from all this crap and to reclaim our lives?" Anna said.

Later, we went to our rooms and rested and then met in the cantina for dinner and afterward sat at the bar. The room was lively and filled with patrons of all types—Mexicans, Americans, Europeans who made it to Rosarito on their itineraries across North America and Mexico.

A mariachi band sent fine lavish chords of music through the room in perfect harmony. Thunderous horns and sweet mandolins and violins. Three men and two women, dressed in red and black and silver costumes and wearing sombreros, sang tales of love and happiness and sorrow. We stayed until late, dancing and drinking.

In the morning, I was the first to come down for breakfast. Soon, Owen arrived, then Anna. Hunched over cups of rich Mexican coffee, we all looked as if the night had drained every drop of life from us. And adding to it, I had a feeling Owen and Anna got little sleep, though I was not about to ask. I suspected that only one of their beds had been used.

# 6

After we returned from Mexico, I did not see Owen for quite a while, though I assumed he was still in San Diego as I knew he would not leave without stopping by.

Progress on my book came slowly. Each morning I was lucky to grind out a thousand words. But I liked the story. It was a good strong tale.

I told my agent I was moving at a steady if slow pace and that I would likely have a draft in a couple of months. It was enough to keep her happy though, in truth, I was beginning to wonder if I was one of those writers who has only one book in them: Harper Lee with *To Kill a Mockingbird*, or J. D. Salinger with *The Catcher in the*

*Rye*. Of course, nothing I had written could match either of those books. I knew my first book was good though it had yet to survive the test of time. Would anyone still be reading it five years from now? Ten years from now?

I started working early in the morning and on most days by one o'clock I was in one of the good restaurants—Jakes or The Poseidon—on the waterfront where I would have a fine lunch of fresh fish, sitting on the veranda overlooking the beach and watching the sun burn away the last of the morning fog.

I wondered if Owen and Anna had been right. Maybe the thing to do was pick up and head to some place new. After all, I was not a person with deep roots—it could be argued barely any at all. It was merely a good and solid wanderlust that pushed me bullishly through life, each time landing me with much uncertainty at my new destination. A solemn yet thin motivation that had forced me to move from Chicago to Boston, and from Boston to San Diego.

Sipping a dry vodka martini while sitting at

The Poseidon, I made a tally of the places in Mexico that were good for expats. I knew which were best and had visited most of them at one time or another. The list was simple. Querétaro, Mérida, Oaxaca, Puerto Vallarta, San Miguel de Allende, Guadalajara, San Felipe, San Luis Potosi. Any would work for what I needed.

I watched the surfers as they headed with alluring eagerness across the sand for their ecclesiastical rendezvous with the sea. The morning fog now all but gone, the sky gleamed in shades of bright and dark cobalt blue as though filtered through the large round stained-glass windows of the cathedrals in Paris and Chartres.

Oddly and for no apparent reason, I found myself thinking about Mercedes—one of those curious surprises that our hippocampus springs on us. I wondered what she had been doing the past seven years. The last time I heard from her she told of her decision to get married—a decision that sounded stiff but resolute. She would marry a lawyer just as Anna had done. I hoped it had turned out better for Mercedes than for Anna.

Yes, I had told Owen that I hardly ever thought about Mercedes anymore. And mostly, it was true. Yet, the excoriation I felt when I found out about her plans forced me into a long, numb state of denial.

I ate my meal, sole meunière, rather dutifully and with little enthusiasm. When I got home, I lay in the hammock in the backyard. A cool breeze that found its way through the branches of the fruit trees and the bushy avocado tree lulled me to sleep. Almost immediately a dream came across me.

The four of us were sitting in a café. I could not tell where except I knew I had been there before. The day was warm. Our table looked onto the ocean—a strong and powerful ocean with a turbid surf. Many young boys and girls zipped across the waves on dazzling surf boards. In an instant, the sea turned cherry red. Many fish—all dead—floated to shore. Anna wanted to go surfing. Then we were out in the plains of Africa. Lions and hyenas hunched near us crouching and watching. A dozen elephants were behind us. A large snake, pink, with horns and the scales of fish twirled between our legs. Before I knew it, I was in a dark dimly lit room. It was cramped and cool and warm all at once. I lay in bed. A door opened. A man stood in the doorway. "I love you, Jack," he said, and closed the door and left.

I sprung awake and slowly pulled my legs over onto the edge of the hammock and sat up— palms wet, brow moist. I sat there for a long while.

Needing to rid myself of the tormenting dream, I went in the house and changed into shorts and a t-shirt and running shoes and set out for a long run along the beach or perhaps down Camino Del Mar and up the sharp hill that rose to Torrey Pines and circle back to the house. Often, I did this to clear out a troublesome thought that haunted me, though on that day it only served to fuse the bleak image of Big Hank in my mind.

Shambling hot and sweaty into the backyard, I found Owen sitting leisurely in a chair with his legs stretched out.

"Thought you might have left…given up on

the good life forever, packed it in and checked out." He laughed and said, "Christ, I've been here an hour."

I explained the dream and my need for a long run, which as it turned out did little good.

"But at least it purged my body of the effects of the two martinis I had at lunch," I said.

"Just two?"

"Two were enough. They probably sent the bad dream to me. Should have stopped at one."

"Or maybe three," Owen declared.

"Yes, maybe three."

I wiped a towel over my face and fell hard into a chair.

"How's the book going?" Owen said.

"Like shit," I said, as I stared at the flagstone beneath me, rubbing my face in the towel.

"It will come. Isn't that what you always used to say when you worked at the *Sun*? When you were having problems with an article?"

"That was different…that was newspaper crap. Now I fooled myself into thinking I can be a writer of fiction," I droned.

Ah, when it comes, it will be better than you expected. Am I correct?"

I nodded slowly as if wanting to believe him.

Owen told me what he had been up to. I was glad to listen, glad to put aside thoughts of the book.

"I spent several days at Anna's over in Rancho Santa Fe. Let me tell you, it's a damn mansion, the place she has."

"So that's where you've been holed up."

"Damn near a week."

"Figured as much."

"Funny thing but Anna is just like she was when I left. It's odd, I think, because we usually change, we all do over time. Isn't that true? But there's something about Anna. She always seems to know who she is. Who she wants to be. She's not like me. Hell, I can't stay the same for twenty minutes."

Owen had that nailed—though it was both a blessing and a curse for him. I had never known a person like Owen, someone who shifted to the moment as he did. Me, I was somewhere situated between Anna and Owen. Once I made up my mind, I usually stuck to it. Yet I could be lulled away without much effort at times.

"We had a damn good time. And I even got along with her two kids, Danny and Sophie. Never thought that was possible. You know me and kids and all," Owen said.

He got up and went into the house and treated both of us to a bottle of beer from my refrigerator.

"Yeah, we got along wonderfully, me and Anna and the kids," Owen said. He tilted the beer to his mouth. "She told me about the guy she married. The guy she divorced. Sam something-or-other. He did corporate junk for quite a while and then he gave it up and started chasing ambulances. Cleaned up real big on the personal injury crap…the heavy-hitting stuff, the multimillion-dollar stuff. Anna said he was good at it because he had no scruples…the guy could sell stink to a skunk, she told me. He knew how to dazzle the jury. And then when he was rolling high on the hog, he started messing around with some "cunt", as she put it. He thought he could snooker Anna the way he did a jury. He thought he was immune to trouble…that he could get away with anything. Guess he didn't really know Anna all that well." Owen tittered gleefully. He slid back in his chair, drank beer, and belched. "You know, Jack, I've just about made up my mind to dump the whole thing with *Time*. Sure, it's been good but…."

"Life evolves."

"Isn't that the damn truth." Owen uttered, looking to the sky. "Anyway, I'm thinking about maybe coming back to Southern California. Maybe it will work out with Anna and me. Can't say it will, but you never know. And most of all, I like her idea about finding some place to live where the pace is slower and easier and, well, with less garbage to deal with. She'll never need to make another nickel again as long as she lives. And me, well I've got a few ducats tucked away. Anna and I talked a lot about it and she seems to have bought into it quite a bit already. Hell, I've always been an expat at heart."

I told Owen about my thoughts of leaving Del Mar for a while.

"What's that you said recently? When it comes down to it we're all a restless bunch, we Americans." He gave that some thought. "Ah, shit, maybe it's better that way. Restless, I mean. It's sort of recharges our batteries so we can keep going. That's how I like to think about it."

I agreed and told Owen that maybe it would be good for me to get away. "Have you decided where?" I asked.

"Anna's got a pretty good short list."

"She was always good at planning, if I remember."

"Yes, and never leaves a stone unturned. I always envied that, me being the impulsive SOB I am."

I laughed a little. "I remember how it drove you a bit nuts at times…the way she plans out everything."

"And it still kind of does…but this time it makes good sense. She's got the list narrowed down to five or six places. And I added a few as well. She's leaning heavy toward Mexico."

"It's easy and close."

"I still think she'd like Italy."

"Italy is a fine place all right. I like it but my Italian is poor, not nearly as good as my Spanish," I said.

"It comes once you're there a while."

"Well, the Italian women are damn beautiful, that's for sure."

"Damn beautiful!"

"Anna's been to Italy…went with Sam. So, she has a good sense of the place. But I think she's still stuck on Mexico. She found a place on the east coast of the Yucatan near a small village called San Rafael."

"I know it. It's on the water."

"Yeah, right on the coast. Good fishing, they say. We'll get ourselves a boat and head out on the water every day. What could be better?"

"Jesus, that sounds swell, all right. I'm liking this more every minute," I said, swiping the towel over the back of my neck and forehead.

"Anna looked in to renting a couple of

places. She got some prices and there are two that sound perfect for what we want. Both sit on a low cliff over the water."

I slumped down in the chair. "I like the Caribbean. It's nice and the water is warm and calm and clear. Good for fishing like you said…and for diving…scuba."

"What do you think? Think you could work there…you know, write?"

"Probably," I said. "If I can't I'll blame you."

"What about Chloe?"

"So, did Anna send you here with this huge list?"

"There, see how thorough she is?"

"I don't know. I'll bounce it off Chloe and see what she thinks. She's got a pretty good network of contacts set up here. They like her work, and they always peddle her stuff in their galleries."

"Check with her anyway, pal. It would be great to have all four of us together there. Don't you think?"

"Shit, that'd be grand. So long as we don't drive each other batshit nuts," I said.

"And you know we will, of course," Owen answered with a hard and deep laugh.

An ambush of purple and pale pink stole the sky as the sun moved to the west. We killed off a few more Corona.

# PART 2

# 1

The house—a yellow stucco two-story affair with good windows all around—sat on a small loft of a hill on the east coast of the Yucatan. From the house you could see quite a way offshore and you knew from its age it had survived many storms. On most days, the Caribbean was as blue as the sky and was always accompanied by a soft and flowery breeze. It was a perfect house for Chloe and me, and was only a short distance away from where Owen and Anna and Sophie and Danny lived.

Farther down the coast was the village of San Rafael, simple, humble, and with all the necessities of life: a modest but adequate grocery, a fine mercado with fresh fruit and vegetables and breads and desserts, three decent restaurants, and a school that was ideal for Sophie and Danny with classes taught in English and Spanish. There were two cantinas—Pablo's and Manny's—one church, a small zocalo, a *tortierilla*, and a fish monger. Tacos and tortas of chicken or pork could be had from street vendors for a few pesos.

I had worked all morning and was happy with what I had accomplished. From the window in front of my desk I could see the waves of the undulating sea. If the day held up, there would be time to take the boat out and fish.

I had bought a cabin cruiser that I kept moored in front of the house. Hardly a day went by when Owen and I did not take it to sea.

"What are you writing?" a voice behind me said.

I turned. "Well…a book, Sophie. I hope so anyway. You surprised me. I didn't hear you come in."

"My mother says I walk too softly. Is it a book I can read?"

"I hope so…someday probably."

"Will I like it?"

"I certainly hope so."

"Tell me what it's about, then maybe I can get my mother to buy it."

"Well, it's not finished yet."

"Is that why you work here every morning?"

"Yes…it takes a long time to write a book."

"Is the book about us?"

"Sort of. But when you write a book, you don't always write about yourself."

"Why do you write books?" Sophie asked.

It was a good question and I had to think about it for a second. "Well, people write books because they think they have something to tell people."

"Is that why you write?"

"Yes, I suppose so."

"Do you like to write?"

I laughed. "Sometimes…yes. But you see, sometimes it can be very difficult."

"But if you have a story that other people like, isn't it easy then?"

I laughed again. "Well, you see, you don't

know if people will like it."

"Then why don't you write a book that people *will* like?"

"Now, that's a grand idea, Sophie. I'll remember it."

"Then everyone will buy it. Will that make you famous…if people like buy your book and like it?

"Sometime, yes."

"Well, I hope you're very famous. Then I can say I know someone who is famous and who writes books. Is it a book that children can read?"

"When they grow up, probably?"

"Does it have pictures?"

"No, just words."

Sophie frowned and said, "I like lots of pictures. I can read very well. I could read almost since I was three years old, a little bit anyway. Now I'm four."

"It is very good that your mother taught you to read at an early age."

"And now I am learning Spanish."

"This is very good, too."

"My mother said I should not come down the street and talk with you when you are working, if you are by the window and looking out at the sea. Does it help if you look at the sea when you write books?"

"It helps a lot."

"My brother Danny is at home. He's still working on his schoolwork, but I finished mine. I do better in school than he does even though he's a year older than I am. I told my mother that someday I will become a writer like you because if you're a writer you don't have to go to work. You can just sit and look at the sea."

"Ha, yes, looking at the sea helps you to think," I said.

"And I told her I will write my books in Spanish because more people speak Spanish."

"Yes, that's true, here anyway."

"So why don't you write your books in Spanish?"

"I should…you're right. But my Spanish is not so good."

"Will you go fishing in your boat today?"

"Yes, it's possible."

"With Owen? Are you going to go with Owen? He lives with us."

"Yes, Owen and I are good friends. And your mother, too. We are all good friends. And Chloe, too."

"I like Chloe. She makes nice pictures. What will you do if you catch some fish?"

"Well, remember last time. We brought them back and cooked them on the grill."

"Yes, I remember. It was very good. I like fish probably more than anything else. Will you get some fish like the ones we had last time?"

"We'll try."

"I need to go now. My mother will wonder where I am."

"That's a good idea. We don't want her getting worried."

"Bye."

"Bye, Sophie."

I printed my work from the day and leaned back in the chair and propped my feet on the desk and read what I had written, then got up and stretched and went to the front of the house and breathed the midday air that curled in from across the sea. As I walked barefoot in the water my toes landed on an oyster shell. I rinsed it and pried it open with my pocketknife and enjoyed the briny treat.

In a short while, Owen came down the path wearing a loose-fitting linen shirt, beige in color, and tan cargo shorts, and deck shoes, and a white Panama hat. "I heard from a terribly reliable source that you are planning to go fishing," he said.

"You have excellent sources. I suppose it is why you were good at *Time*."

"And she said you are writing a book." Owen quipped. "Such secrets you keep."

"Right on both accounts."

"And she said you live with someone who paints wonderful pictures, and I certainly believe it because this person—my secret source—she never stretches the truth. And better yet, she said you are planning to go fishing and come back with something excellent for dinner tonight."

"Yes, I have a good feeling we will come back with something good for dinner."

"Always trust your hunches," Owen declared. "Have you gassed up the boat?"

"Yesterday when we got back."

"Then we should go before it gets too hot. The fish get lazy in the afternoon."

The sun was already large and white, with a few clouds as transparent as lace.

I loaded the equipment onto the boat. Owen turned on the engines and set the boat to the sea and directed it along the coast and pulled to a stop at Cedro's Bait Shop.

"What will it be today, Señor Jack?" Cedro asked, coming quickly out to the boat.

"Something good for snapper and grouper…and whatever else is out there."

"*Si!* Delicious chunks of bonita I have…oily and smelly."

He came back with a plastic bucket of bonita.

"They look good. Your bonita are the best bait."

"The fish love them because they are oily and smelly."

"Yes, very oily and smelly," I said.

"The fish out there will not resist zees very delicious bonita," Cedro said.

"We always catch good fish with your bait, Cedro," I said. "That's why we come here every day."

"I hope you continue to, Mr. Jack."

"*Cuánto?*" I said.

Cedro shrugged. "Oh, *no mucho*. Maybe *diez*," he said with a friendly shrug.

I handed him a bill.

"You do well out there now," Cedro called as we pulled off.

"Where to today?" Owen said, feeding the throttle.

"You decide. You seem to have figured out where the fish are hiding at this time of day."

"Luck of the Irish, that's all" Owen declared.

"Thought you were a Hoosier," I said.

"An Irish Hoosier," Owen said. He turned

the boat east into the Caribbean. "Over there," pointing to a dark blue patch of sea at about ten o'clock, swinging the boat thirty degrees to the left.

"Yes, if I remember we had good success there a while back. I glanced over the side of the boat at the sandy and rocky bottom in the clear water below. I reached down and caught a spray of water, cool and warm both. It felt good to be away from the land, separated from my morning work. The sea always brought a dose of mental freedom, like talking to a good friend and feeling refreshed afterwards.

"Did you check the weather?" Owen called over his shoulder, knowing of course that I had.

"Twice. It will be fine, minus a squall perhaps. But we can't worry about that. They come and go and never last long. Say, how's your feeling about going in with the spears? I have them in the cabin."

Owen balked. "Lots of Corona last night. Let me think it over." He angled the boat due east. "And Anna wore me out, too"

"Sounds like everything is fine, then?"

"Damn good. We did the right thing, leaving California I mean. Funny, isn't it, Jack, you never really know if you're making the right decision until you do it. You think it's a good choice, but it might turn out to be damn rotten. The kids— Sophie and Danny—are in a good school, and that makes Anna happy more than anything. You wouldn't think so, but I'm getting used to them. They're sort of fun. Full of questions. Especially Sophie."

"So I learned."

"Were we like that as kids," Owen wondered.

"All kids are like that, I think."

"And the money for them is still coming in from Sam. We'll see how long that lasts. Anna said as soon as the bastard finds out about us, he'll try to cut her off. She's ready for it, though. She's got that lawyer friend of hers all set to jump on his ass."

We hadn't gone far when Owen pointed to his left, "Oh, Christ, now will you look at *that*."

I turned in time to see the tail of a fish slip into the water.

"Helluva a big grouper. It's a good sign. Says, there is a lot still going on down there. They haven't given up on lunch yet, I guess." He turned the boat a few degrees in the direction.

"They need to stay hungry enough for oily bonita we brought."

"Don't worry, they won't be able to resist the bonita. You'll see," Owen said.

When we got to the patch of blue sea, Owen cut the engine and let the boat drift and bob.

"Let's at least see what's going on down there. What do you say, old boy?" I said. I reached for the snorkels and masks and fins.

Owen nodded unenthusiastically.

"It'll clean you head." I said, to which I got no reply. I dropped anchor. "A good twenty-five. Just right for what we're after today."

We climbed down a small ladder into the water. It was warm with a slight chill. I spit into my mask and rubbed it on the lens and rinsed it and then slipped the mask over my head and pressed it to my face. Looking into the water, I could easily see the sandy bottom and a small ridge of coral that precipitated into a break on the flat sea floor.

Fish of all sizes hovered near the coral or moved obliquely this way and that, keeping distance from each other. I cleared my mask again and then followed Owen, who pointed to a nice sized grouper that weaved lonely near the bottom. Flounder, too. Out in front of us, a small school of snapper swept effortlessly through the water, turning sharply and pulling away as we came near.

A lone barracuda with a mouth full of irregular pinpoint fangs and a thin body and pair of dorsal fins paid a visit to the coral ridge, moving almost motionless along the ocean floor, waiting for a foolish fish to pull in close. I watched for the ever-present sharks, especially the aggressive and unpredictable bull sharks, but I knew the fish themselves would be good sentinels for them. They never hung around long when a bull was near.

Now I was sorry we did not grab the spear-guns on our way into the water. I waved to Owen at a fish. He pretended to aim an imaginary spear-gun as it coasted dangerously close to us.

Back on the boat, I took the rods, gave one to Owen, and opened the bait bucket. It was certain we would need to get a line in the water soon if we had any hopes of bringing in dinner. We hooked a choice piece of bonita onto our lines and dropped them into the water.

I tucked the long handle tightly under my right arm and grasped the rod with my left hand and worked the jenny with my right. When I felt the bait settle to the floor, I raised it a trace and let the motion of the boat pull it slowly along. Owen kept his line about halfway to the bottom, hoping to tempt a snapper.

In time, we had a few quick strikes. I reeled my line in. "Ah, the bastard is a damn good thief, all right," I said, looking at the bare hook.

Owen chuckled. "See, they are a hell of a lot smarter than we think."

"Not for long," I declared, lowering another

chunk of bonita into the water. In almost no time I felt another jerk and then the line went loose. "Son-of-a-bitch," I groaned. "I think we found the smartest bunch of fish in the sea."

"Or the dumbest fishermen." As soon as Owen said that the tip of his rod bent sharply down. "Aha…*here* we go now!"

He let the fish swim, reeling in gradually and playing it as it circled out and came back.

"It's not a giant, that's for sure…but it has lots of spirit."

It circled again, and twice more. Each time heading away then returning in a wide arc.

"Okay, I'll bring it over this way," Owen said.

As it came by, I slipped a net under.

"A damn good snapper, all right" I said. "Won't get anything as fresh as this from the monger in town, that's for damn sure. We'll need one more to feed the six of us. You know Sophie. She can eat a lot of fish. She told me so."

"If Sophie said it, you can believe it," Owen crowed.

I baited up and dropped my line in. "I think you've got the right idea, old boy. To hell with the grouper…go for the snapper. One more and we'll have a swell meal tonight."

We kept at it, doing little more than merely feeding the fish with our bonita all the while.

"If this keeps up, may have to go to lures," I said.

"Lures are all right. We had good luck with them in the past."

I looked into the bucket. "A couple more smelly bonita and out go the lures." I had barely finished speaking when my line dipped fast into the sea. "Okay, this bastard's not getting away," I said, setting the hook.

When we got it in the boat, Owen said, "Ah yes, this will feed us tonight."

We continued with catch-and-release for a while and then threw the remaining few pieces of bonita into the sea. We turned for the shore just as the sharp, sleek fin of a bull shark announced its presence.

"No point hanging around with that fella

here," Owen said, taking the wheel and pushing the throttle.

I cleaned the fish on shore and put the fillets in the refrigerator, and then climbed into a hammock for the rest of the afternoon. I thought about my book. I always thought about it off and on during the day. Some writers say they can empty out the thoughts of what they're working on after they're done for the day. Maybe it's true. I don't know. But having cut my teeth as an ink slinger for tabloids, I could rarely do that. Writing then was a never-ending process of pecking out the words until the story was done, turning it over to the editors, and starting again on another piece. Regardless, the book was moving along fine and I was happy with it. I could be content with that for now.

When we moved to Mexico, I told my agent I had decided to leave Del Mar and go there with a couple of friends, and that we had a house by the sea, and that it was a nice place to work. That it was quiet and that the ocean always fed me with good thoughts. And that I was able to make progress on the book. She worried I would stall or would get distracted and slow down, or that I might even quit the project all together. Agents were like that I learned. Persistent, pushy, worrisome bastards with only one thing on their mind. They seemed to think we, writers, were nothing more than their drudges and that we should keep plowing forward no matter what. Of course, being the independent cuss I was, none of that really mattered to me.

Later Chloe and I went to the house shared by Owen and Anna and had a delightful dinner of the fish that Owen and I had caught that day. A kind and pampering breeze drifted around the backyard.

After dinner, Anna said, "So, Jack hasn't mentioned a word about his book in a long time and now I'm getting awfully curious."

I shrugged and dodged the question with a sip of wine.

"It's bad luck to talk about it," Chloe said. "Or that's what he always says. And I can tell you, Jack is superstitious as hell."

"You can't trust your work until you're done," I said. "Words are tricky. And even a good story, if you think you have one, can turn out to be a total flop."

"*Well*…he told me all about his book this morning," Sophie announced with a burst of swagger.

"Oh, *really*?" Anna sparked. "Well, now, don't keep us in suspense."

"Yes, he said it has *words* but no *pictures*. And that it takes a very *long* time to write a book. And that you need a window to look out of."

"We have lots of windows here in our house," Danny said. "Maybe you should write over here. We have so many windows you could write really fast and maybe finish the book in a day, or maybe even an hour."

"And then he'll just have to start another book, *Danny*," Sophie tartly said to her brother, hands on her hips.

"Or he could take his boat out and go fishing," Danny said.

"I already told him that, Danny," Sophie

croaked.

"Well, those are all good ideas. It always helps when people come up with good ideas to help you out," I said.

"Okay now, a toast to all the good ideas," Owen said. He held up his glass. "And by the way, *this* is a very good wine, all right."

"There's a shop in the village. I discovered it the other day when I was there. It's down a block or so from the zocalo. They have an excellent selection of French," Anna said.

"Is it a *helluva* good wine?" Sophie asked.

"So-*phie*…how many times have I told you."

"But that's what they always say, Owen and Jack. They always say—"

"I don't care. Mind your tongue," Anna said.

"I *told* you Mom would say that," Danny declared, rather delighted.

"Anyway, I want to talk about other things," Anna said.

"Like what?" Sophie said, with an edge of

disappointment.

"Like Chloe's paintings maybe…or Owen's photography…or, yes, Jack's book even. If *that's* okay with you, Sophie."

Sophie puffed her cheeks and said, "Ooh-kay."

"My, you're getting impertinent,' Anna said.

"I don't know what impermanum means," Sophie replied.

"Good!" Anna said. "And now that dinner is over, I suggest both of you go in and finish your homework."

"We already did. Can we watch TV?" Sophie asked.

Chloe looked at Anna and laughed. "Have you seen TV here in Mexico? It's nothing but a bunch of soap operas."

"What's that?" Sophie asked.

"Never mind," Anna said. "Scoot…into the house now and get ready for tomorrow."

"Bye," they said simultaneously and took off to the back door.

"Oh, Lord, what a handful!" Anna said. "Remember when we were in college and they talked about nature-versus-nurture in Psych 101? Well, I've got the answer right here. Sophie is Sam all the way. And Danny is me in every way. Sophie's got that never-give-an-inch persistence that Sam had. And Danny, well Danny is mister-go-along-to-get-long. Sophie will drive you to drink sometimes." Anna picked up her glass. "So, cheers!"

"Sometimes I think kids know more about life than we do, it's just that they don't realize it," Chloe said. "You know, the way they put every-thing together one piece at a time is what I mean. Sometimes when I'm painting, I think about that—the way a painting is built up on the canvas in layers. And yet, life is like that, too. It's just one layer added to the next, and to the next, and…." Chloe sat back and shook her head. "Oh, crap, I'm getting much too philosophical now! Must be that helluva good wine Anna found in town."

"Then be sure you buy more," I told Anna.

*

In the morning I sent an email to my agent. I figured I had better assuage her fears. I said the book was moving along well, which was mostly true, and that with luck I would have my first draft in a month, maybe two. Though I was not happy with everything I had written, I did not tell her that, probably because I was never fully satisfied with the words I put on the page. This was even true for my first book, yet now more than three years later it was still riding high on the charts—*The New York Times*, Amazon, and all the others—and the royalties were coming in strong and steady.

Having finished my writing for the day—as much as the muse would permit, at least—I sat and looked out the window at the aqua sea as it rose and sank in endless motion.

Were we happy to have left the US and to have come to San Rafael, I wondered…the four of us, well the six of us? Sophie and Danny were happy, that I could tell. That's how it always went, though. Kids make their home wherever they are. We adults, we always scrutinize, always compare, always endlessly review our decisions, our situations, our circumstances. Is it because we imagine we can change them, our decisions, if they are not what we had hoped for? I watched Sophie and Danny. They lived for today, never for yesterday, rarely for tomorrow. Adults live for tomorrow…rarely for today. Why? What was it about tomorrow that seemed better than what we had today?

I thought about the time we had now spent in Mexico. Expats? What does that really mean? Does it mean we will never go back? Never again tolerate the life we left? Never be content? The constant search for something better. Had we now found that "something better" for which we were searching? Yet, I realized that when you give up one life and replace it with another, it is merely an alteration, not a change. There is little about life we can inherently change.

This was the recurrent dilemma that kept coming back to me and I knew that it was the very essence, the marrow, of what drove me through life. Odd, my new book was about the four of us even though I told Sophie it wasn't. What else is there to write about than what you know—than what you have experienced?

I looked at the books by Patrick Modiano that I kept stacked clumsily on the corner of my desk. Modiano—the Nobel laureate of recent years who wrote about his endless journey into the contentious way the mind, with its insoluble memory, surreptitiously hides from us the most irksome parts of our past. All writers worth their salt looked inward into their own lives, their own failures, their own successes. Or, at the least, to the lives and experiences of those who surrounded them.

Yes, life in Mexico was simple and pleasant. So, perhaps we truly had found what we sought. Life had become slower because there was no way to speed it up. No mental escalators carrying us recklessly up and down through life—it had its own centrifugal clutch that disengaged when the foot was taken from the pedal.

In California it was not possible to

disengage the clutch; the gears kept spinning and turning. Even when we thought we had stepped off the never-ending escalator, life required many brakes just to temper its exhausting pace a little. Here, life had its own simple and satisfying pace. Was it what I wanted? Or was it merely life masquerading as something else? I was never going back to that other life. So I believed.

# 2

The days moved quietly along. I worked for several hours every morning, 'looking out the window', as Sophie would say. Afternoons on the sea. In the water with spears or fishing from the boat.

Life was good and even Chloe, whom I worried would find the change too much of an adjustment and might hunger for Del Mar, liked her new life on the coast of the Caribbean as much as the rest of us did. It had opened a new dimension to her art, and I could see the happiness it brought to her.

Many years ago when I left the orphanage and traveled the world, I came to know that happiness is a fickle emotion. It is like the sea breeze that we never know when it will come and when it will stop. Just when we think we have found happiness, life again deals a crappy hand—a hand with nothing but ones and twos and devoid of face cards, and then we must struggle to make something of it. But as Jack London adroitly put it: "Life is not a matter of holding good cards, but sometimes playing a bad hand well". I often thought of that when I looked forlornly at a nasty hand I had suddenly acquired.

But now, as had happened many times in my life, I seemed to have been given kings and queens and a few high cards as well, and I gratefully accepted that.

One afternoon, Owen came by as I was finishing up for the day.

"Got a minute, Jack?" he said as we stood out by the water. "I have something important to tell you."

"Of course, old boy. What's up?"

"To Pablo's," he said, nodding to town.

"That important, huh?"

The cantina was nearly empty when we arrived. A few locals at the bar. One or two tables with expats, faces we were beginning to recognize. The dark room was seeded with music from a pair of good speakers. Pablo stood lazily behind the bar.

"Tequila," I said. "Something respectable."

Pablo poured two long shots of Petrón.

I leaned on the bar, picked up the glass, and pulled in a small sip. "So, what's the big secret?" I said.

"I got a call from *Time*."

"Thought you retired."

"So did I. But apparently *Time* thinks otherwise. There is a skirmish going on in Chiapas. We've all heard about it for quite a while now."

"I've been trying not to pay attention," I said. "Thought we came here to escape from the world."

"Well, the magazine wondered if we can get over and see what's going on."

"They seem to be keeping good tabs on you. How the hell did they find you?"

"Sources…I guess. Anyway, I had a long phone call with Ted Bauer. He was an editor of mine at the magazine. He wants to know if we can help him out…make a trip over to Chiapas and see what's happening. He knows about your work; he thought we could pair up and snoop around Chiapas. It turns out there is a group up in the hills that are causing trouble for the government and the local farmers, the banana and coffee ranchers. That's what Bauer heard. The government is concerned it could escalate into a big problem for them. There is someone up in the hills the magazine wants us to get a story from."

"What about the expat thing? Sort of blows that to hell, don't you think?

"Not for good. There will still be plenty of time for the sea when we get back. But now, tell me the truth, Jack, aren't you just a little antsy for some action? Maybe it's just in my blood. You know what I mean…the action and all."

I shrugged and sipped the musky liquor but did not commit to Owen's notion. "Pretty good sauce," I said. "I could get used to this stuff."

"Well, anyway, it's just a short assignment from what I can tell. Then we can return to our nice lazy life back here. We can take Anna's Land Rover to Chiapas."

"Where in Chiapas?"

"Not sure…up in the hills."

"Always up in the hills, eh?"

"The magazine will let us know. They're anxious to find out what's going on. They want to get in on it first."

I thought about my book. Could I put it on hold for a while? I was finally making progress, but a couple of weeks wouldn't matter. Sometimes a break helps.

"It should be an easy assignment," Owen said. "Nothing more than a chat with a couple of people, a few photos. The kind of stuff we can do in our sleep. Easy."

"Nothing's easy anymore, old boy."

Bauer thought a few days is all it will take. Just get a story, write it up, that's pretty much it." Owen breathed the flavor of the tequila and took a drink. "Nice stuff," he said. "Nice stuff. I guess if nothing else we can thank Bauer for a visit to Pablo's."

"What do you know about the situation?"

"Not much. But I learned to live with that when I worked for the magazine. It usually went like this: 'Owen, get on a plane to Morocco. We'll fill you in when you get there…or along the way'. Anyway, it has to do with a group up in the hills. The natives and peasants, I think. That's all I know."

"Yes, yes. The same old story in Mexico for a couple hundred years now. Screw the natives…take their land. Isn't that how it goes?"

Music played. The cantina was slowly filling with expats who came in for the good tequila and to hide from the brilliant midday sun. A woman got up and fed pesos into the jukebox. Fleetwood Mac, *Don't Stop Thinking About Tomorrow*. An odd rejoinder, I thought, for anyone who came to San Rafael to avoid thinking about tomorrow. Ah, but how ineffectively we cover our tracks even from ourselves.

Owen signaled to Pablo for a refill.

"Nice ploy," I said, sipping the liquor. "One more of these and you'll have me in the water taking on a mean-ass bull with a spear gun.”

Owen immediately grabbed the image and laughed exuberantly.

“Well, I’m still worried about abandoning our plans of leaving all the crap we wanted to get away from,” I said. “Isn’t that why we came here? And look at us now, here we are planning to escape into the hills to get a handle on what’s going on there for some wretched magazine.”

“I’m with you, Jack, I am. Believe me I am,” Owen said. “We can do this, just this once, and then we’ll come back to life as we know it. Cross my heart.”

“And hope to die?”

Now it was Garcia and Grisman, *Sitting Here in Limbo*. All I could do was laugh.

“When does he want an answer?” I asked. “This Bauer fella?”

“Always yesterday. That’s how the weeklies work. Always yesterday.”

“And what about Anna?”

“She’s okay with it. What will Chloe say?”

I shrugged and turned away for a second,

then said, "Not sure. She treats me like a king, you know that. I'm a damn lucky bastard."

"All we really need to do is throw a few things in the Land Rover and head over to Chiapas."

The music shifted to Mexican ballads. Pablo tossed ice into a blender of margaritas and turned it on. People continued to stroll into the cantina. The open windows fed the room with wonderful smells of the midday Mexican village: pinto beans simmering in kitchens, fresh fish tacos from the street vendors. A pair of ceiling fans turned in slow endless motion. More expats came in. They were always easy to spot—tanned, ruffled hair, shorts, sandals, t-shirt or the Cuban wedding shirts you see up and down the Yucatan.

I knew I would not be able to resist Owen's request to make a trip over to Chiapas, and I knew that if I were to do that, he would go on his own anyway. More so, I knew that neither of us had slipped so far into the expat thing yet that we couldn't slip out just as easily.

"I'll mention it to Chloe and see what she

says. I'll throw the decision in her lap. And of course, she will throw it back in mine."

"Then we go."

"Huh! Must be the Patrón," I murmured.

"We'll leave in the morning," Owen replied. He held up his glass of Tequila. "Chiapas."

# 3

I spent the evening gathering what I needed for the trip and packed a small duffle of clothes and placed my laptop safely inside and got a couple hours of sleep.

In the morning, as the sun came in from over the sea, we loaded the Land Rover with clothes and equipment and a large jug of water. Anna and Chloe and Sophie and Danny stood next to the car. I saw an uncomfortable look on Anna's face that she managed to hide with reasonable success.

"Where are you going?" Sophie said.

"On a short trip," I told her.

"Are you coming back?" she daintily asked.

"Hush, Sophie," Anna said firmly. "Of

course, they're coming back."

"That's right, dear. We'll be back before you can say pumpkin pie," Owen said.

"Why should I say pumpkin pie?"

"Go ahead, say it."

"Pumpkin pie."

"See…we're back."

Sophie frowned. "You didn't even go."

"Now, you just wait, we'll be back in no time at all," I said.

"How far are you going?" Sophie asked.

"A couple hundred miles," I said.

"Is that far away?"

"Not so much. We'll drive the car,"

"But the roads down here suck. That's what Mom said. She said they're crappy."

"Sophie," Anna said.

"We'll only take the good ones. How's that?" Owen said.

"You ask too many questions, Sophie," Anna said.

"What will you do when you get there?" Sophie asked.

"Talk to some people and write a story," Owen replied.

"Can't you talk to them from here on your phone?"

"No, not really. We need to be there. Besides, I need to take some photographs," Owen said.

"You just wait…we will be back in no time at all," I said.

"Will you go fishing in your boat when you get back?"

"Of course, sweetheart. Of course, we will. Every single day," Owen said.

"What if all the fish get bored and go someplace else?"

"Jack and Owen need to move along," Anna said.

"Now you and Danny stay here with Anna and Chloe…and do your schoolwork…and listen to your mother. Okay?" Owen said.

"—kay."

I waved to the group from the window as we took to the road.

Owen said Bauer had sent him a text late at night telling us to go to a place called Billie Carrigan's Pub in Tuxtla. Once there we were to ask for a man named Montego. He would give us direction up in the hills where we would find a man named Martinez. Bauer told Owen that Martinez was the engine that drove the whole operation. There was a price on his head. The government knew if they could take out Martinez, the mission would be crippled. *Time* wanted interviews and photos of Martinez and his *campaneros*.

Within an hour we were moving down Hwy 307 along the coast of Quintana Roo past the shabby jungle toward Hwy 186, which would take us west to Campeche and then to Tuxtla in Chiapas. It was not all that far, six hundred miles by the crow, twelve hours. But we both knew that distances in Mexico were artificial. Success on the road depended on the traffic. A slow humble car could crush movement for everyone. A peasant bus or an overloaded eighteen-wheeler lumbering along at twenty-five miles an hour up and down the spiny vertebrae of the hills and mountains could bring traffic to a near stop. And, of course, roads torn apart from disrepair—the worst enemy of all.

"With luck, we'll be in Tuxtla this evening," Owen predicted.

"With luck, yes," I said. I glanced at the sky where turkey buzzards circled in silent motion waiting for their chance at the bloody entrails of a hare or opossum along the road. I had a sudden and unaccountable feeling that they were also watching us with the same sharp eyes as we passed across the sodden land.

"We'll wrap this thing up in no time and come back to our grand life in San Rafael," Owen swore. "I told Bauer he's lucky we agreed to do this for him at all."

"Where are all his people in Mexico? Surely, he has someone down here who can do it."

"Tied up with work is what he said. I knew a fellow from when I worked out East who is now in Mexico City. Richard Haspen is his name. Nice guy and good with the lens. A shooter.

Bauer said he's in the middle of a big assignment. In fact, it was Haspen who gave me away. He is the one who knew I'm in Mexico. Ha! You always think you've got yourself covered, but you never really are. I made Bauer promise this would be the last."

"Fat chance. Three months and he'll be back at you. You're stuck now. He's got you tagged, buddy."

"Augh! Christ, look at the mess up ahead." Owen gasped and pointed to a line of cars barely moving. "Some kind of crap going on up there."

We slowed to barely ten miles an hour—stopping and starting. Half a mile up the road, a flatbed truck stacked high with crates of pineapples had slid onto the shoulder. Pineapples everywhere.

"Well, that just added forty-five minutes to our journey," Owen groaned, as we inched down the road and passed the truck. "Want a pineapple?"

We arrived in Tuxtla well after sundown, tired, weary, and in need of a shower and a bed.

We drove to the center of town and got two rooms at a small but pleasant pensión with a nice courtyard and a small restaurant and had a good meal of stewed chicken and cold beer.

The next day we went to Billie Carrigan's Pub—authentic looking but oddly out of place with the rest of the stores, restaurants, cafés, and cantinas in Tuxtla. A simple bar with a half dozen tables covered with checkered oilcloth, one of which had a quartet of gringos seemingly deep in conversation. A man was clearing a table.

"Excuse me, we're looking for Montego," I said. "We were told we could find him here."

"Looking for who?" the man uttered in a flat voice without looking up.

"Montego."

"Montego? And who are you?"

"We were sent here by a magazine in the States. They want us to do a story on Martinez. Montego is expecting us."

The man stopped clearing the table and looked at each of us head to foot. He shrugged and with great indifference returned to the table, saying nothing.

Owen tried again. "We were told Montego would be here,"

"Told by whom?" the man asked in a strong Irish accent.

"*Time* magazine. The magazine we work for."

"And what do they want you to do here?"

"Talk to Montego."

"And who is Montego?"

"We are not sure. We thought you would know. Someone who can help us find Martinez, we were told," Owen said.

"I know everybody who comes in here," the man said. "And they know me." He seemed to try to make it sound like he had no idea who Montego was.

"Well, we're working for *Time* magazine," I repeated.

"We get a lot of people coming in here claiming all kind of shit," the man replied. "It seems to be a sort of game. Go into Billie Carrigan's place and bullshit the other people there.

You know, pretend you're someone you're not. That's why half of them come down here to Mexico…to pretend they're hot shit when in fact they're nothing," he said snidely.

"The magazine is interested in a story about a fellow named Martinez—someone up in the hills here in Chiapas. That's really about all we know."

The man's face hardened. Now I was sure he knew exactly what we were talking about but pretended not to. "Well, I'm Billie Carrigan. I own this pub…this saloon…cantina, if you prefer. You describe it as you like. I don't give a shit," he said with an Irish hum. "A place for ex-pats here in the heart of Mexico. But let's get it straight. I don't give a *daahm* about anyone's politics, if ya care to know. I have no interest in anyone's sacred mission but my own. The expats, they come in here to soak up my tequila and slosh my beer…and to chug down their holy margaritas. That's all I give a shit about. *Understand*?"

"Yes, we understand," Owen said. "But, all we're trying to do is find someone named

Montego, that's all…he has some information for us."

Billie Carrigan shook his head and shrugged impassively again and grabbed a stack of plates and left for the kitchen as though finished with us.

"I've seen this ruse a thousand times," Owen said. "Just wait, he will be back, you'll see. I can tell this Billie Carrigan cat is wedded to this mission as much as anyone. He's a pretty damn lousy liar. Not as good at deception as he thinks he is. He wouldn't let this Montego character anywhere near his *saloon* if he didn't want him here. These Limeys have a soft heart for justice…oh yes. They're trying to wash away the guilt from all the centuries they kept half the world squashed under their thumb."

Billie Carrigan returned from the kitchen and went to the bar and set up drinks for a group of people. I was beginning to wonder if we would ever meet Montego. Finally, after a long while, a light-skinned Latin man with a narrow face and sharp hazel eyes came from the kitchen. He scanned us one by one.

"*Yo soy Montego*," the man said firmly but cautiously, sitting at the table.

Owen talked to him in Spanish that was little better than mine. He showed the man his ID from the magazine and answered a series of questions to confirm proof of that. Finally convinced, the man took us over to a table on the edge of the room and drew a map on a small piece of paper.

"Okay….this is it," he said speaking in English and tapping the paper. "You can get to this road on the edge of town. From there, follow the map as best you can. When you get here," he tapped the map again, "there is the tiny village of San Christi. There, it will be a small restaurant. You will know it by the colors of red and white, and green, the colors of Mexico, painted on it. People there know how to find Martinez. No more can I tell you. You will have to figure it out on your own. That is all. It is a puzzle, and you will have to figure it out. Okay, goodbye." He got up to leave but hesitated and added, "Careful."

I saw Billie Carrigan glance over as

Montego returned to the back room.

We left Billie Carrigan's and started out of town using Montego's crude map. I sent a Text to Chloe and Anna telling them everything was moving along fine and that we were heading out to speak with Martinez.

They both answered immediately telling us to be safe and return home soon.

We had barely reached the outskirts of Tuxtla before the road turned to a poorly-traveled path that rose over one hill after another, each time bringing us higher up. The air chilled as we climbed into the hills. Patches of crops grew haphazardly along the road and onto the hillside— thin and prickly looking stalks of corn each with a few tapered ears. We passed coffee bean ranches with rows of bushes tended by workers who trimmed branches and harvested the deep purple kernels as delicately as though in a French vineyard.

The sky was clear, barely a cloud. Every dozen miles a tiny village of a half dozen adobe huts held tight to the road. Thin wisps of smoke rose from chimneys. An old woman with straight black hair and a dark and wrinkled face, hunched and wearing a tattered poncho, walked along in small steps. A dirty paper sack in her arms. She stopped and watched us pass as though we were a rarity.

We continued on for what seemed like quite a distance even though our progress was consumed by the need to navigate a road that progressively became little more than a footpath as it weaved up and down and around the hills.

At one o'clock we arrived at what appeared to be San Christi. We had no way to be sure, and there were no signs to confirm it. One building, a restaurant, was painted on the side exactly as Montego had described.

"I would guess this is it," Owen said, looking around. "We've been past a bunch of villages, but none like this."

"Not much here. Pretty damn simple," I said.

"As Montego predicted."

Owen parked by the restaurant. We got out.

I stretched my back and my legs that were more stiff than usual. Maybe it was the winding and jutted road that made the trip more difficult. I don't know. I breathed the cool air that carried the scent of wood burning from the restaurant.

We entered what was little more than a crude shack with a couple of tables and a Mexican flag nailed to the wall. A pair of cheap speakers played Christian Nodal. A group of three—a family perhaps—sat to our right, each with a bowl of what could have been *menudo*. A waitress wearing a lively checked apron brought a bottle of beer to the man and returned to the kitchen.

"The way we play this will be important. We have to go easy trying to hook up with Martinez," Owen said. "That's my reading. If I learned anything from my years with the magazine it's that patience pays off. You push it and you lose the whole fucking thing."

"Never knew you to be patient, old boy," I said.

"When I need to…when I need to. Not too

much. Just a little. True, I'm not one of those people who likes to think things over forever."

"Hadn't noticed."

"You need to figure out what's best and what's not. And don't forget. This Martinez fellow and his buddies probably won't be willing to let us just come marching into their operation. They're savvy, damn savvy, or they wouldn't have lasted this long. They won't trust us one damn bit. The CIA is still sticking its damn neck into everything that goes on down here. Be sure of that. Everything! When I worked for the magazine, I spent half my time convincing people I was not a spook for the Company…the CIA. Everyone thinks you're on the other side working against them. You can't win."

"You've got credentials…from the magazine."

"Don't mean nothin' to nobody," Owen uttered succinctly. "Any moron can forge them. Easy to fake. They'll want better proof."

"And if we can't?"

"Bauer knows the odds. I told him we could

end up drilling a dry hole. Come back with nothing at all. He knows the odds."

"Good for that, at least. I for one am not interested in putting my blood into this. I'm no Audie Murphey. I'm a hell of a lot like what Billie Carrigan said at his pub about his commitment to the cause."

"You're more level-headed than I am," Owen said. "I can get stubborn at times like this. Too tied into getting a story at all cost."

"Too tied into staying alive, that's my version of the whole thing."

Owen smiled. I could tell he liked my perspective, and I could tell it probably only served to give him more incentive to keep going.

The waitress with the checked apron came by and handed us a small hand-written menu with no more than a few items on it. We both ordered a torta and beer.

The waitress set two bottles of beer and a bowl of tortilla chips and salsa on the table.

When lunch arrived, Owen raised his beer and said, "*Con mucho gusto, Amigo!* Eat up. No telling when our next meal will come."

"I don't see any chance of getting to Martinez from here. The old lady working the tables doesn't struck me as hardened revolutionary," I said.

"Maybe…maybe not," Owen replied. "These movements can have deep roots." When she returned to the table, Owen presented his ID and explained our desire to meet up with Martinez. She listened to everything he said and merely shook her head and raised her shoulders.

The trio at the table to our right got up. They thanked the waitress and left. As the door closed, almost to the second, she led us to a window and pulled the curtain back two inches and pointed down the street to a small filling station.

"*Alli?*" Owen said.

"*Si,*" she replied, turning quickly to the restaurant again.

We thanked her and paid up and left.

Outside, Owen said, "Montego was right. You need to keep fitting the pieces together one by one until you have the whole picture."

We walked a short distance down the street to the filling station where a man with a round head and straight black hair tied in the back and a thin bristly mustache and a chin with sparse whiskers was repairing a truck tire. We introduced ourselves and delivered the same rather monotonous explanation for our visit.

The man stopped working and wiped his hands on a rag and listened to what we were saying. He looked at the ID Owen presented, but only casually, and feigned indifference and ignorance. I told him we were doing a story for *Time* magazine and that we wanted to talk to Martinez but needed someone to take us to him. The man's eyes moved back and forth as he spoke, his voice dropped almost to a whisper. He backed up and rested an arm on a large truck tire, as if he did not want to be mistaken as an acquaintance of ours, as if the best thing we could do would be to leave. But it was simple to see that he, like all the people we had encountered on our journey to find Martinez, was adding his part to the puzzle.

Montego, apparently, had informed the man

we were coming. The man, speaking quickly and softly, said we could be taken to Martinez that afternoon. He told us to wait in the back room.

"We need our equipment from our vehicle," Owen said to him. "We cannot go without it."

"There will be time," the man said and left.

"Now what?" I said to Owen.

"Sit it out."

"How long?"

"Your guess. Not long probably. They could drag it out to see how we take it. They could. It's possible. I don't think they will, though they might. If they do, we'll know in time. It would mean they don't trust us, and *that's* a big hole to dig out of," Owen said.

"And a great chance to tell Bauer it's a waste of time."

"They won't, though. Drag it out, I mean. You'll see. Usually when you got this far momentum takes over."

There was a long silence until Owen lightly said, "Wonder what Sophie is up to?"

"You like Sophie, huh?"

"Hard not to. She's a ball…sweet little kid."

"Never thought I'd hear you say that."

"Never thought I would." Owen seemed to think about that for a second, then said, "I guess I thought kids were just a lot of trouble and, well, in a sense I suppose they are. But they can make you laugh. Especially the things they say."

"So I have found out."

"I heard she likes to come by and bug you when you're writing."

"Ah, it's fine. And anyway, she seems to know when it's a good time to come by and when it's not. I don't know if Anna told her that. Sofie said she looks at the window to see if I'm working. But I don't think she really does."

"That's what I mean. See, what I've learned is that kids in some ways know more about life than we do," Owen said. "Isn't that crazy. We think because we're older we have some kind of crystal ball that allows us to see everything very clearly."

"What a stupid thought," I replied.

"But we do…we believe it. At least when it

comes to how we view kids."

"Not me. Each year I get stupider and stupider."

Owen chuckled dryly. "Is that a word?"

"You're asking me?"

"Thought you were the writer,"

"Ah…thanks for reminding me. I'll look it up in the dictionary when we get home."

"So, I guess being with Anna and the kids—Sophie and Danny—has kind of changed me. Never thought that was possible."

"That's what I like about you, Owen. You're very philosophical about life."

Owen smiled as though what I said was little more than a cute joke.

"I'm quite serious. You are."

"I know," he said almost remorsefully. "And it will probably be my goddamn downfall someday."

"Nah, you just take it all too seriously, that's all."

"Probably. But how else is there to take it?"

"Well, like when we're trolling for snapper.

That's how," I said.

"That's just when we're out trying to bring home dinner."

"Ah, it's no different."

"Really think so, huh?"

"Damn right."

"Well, people who don't try to figure shit out get stuck in a rut," Owen said. "Look at me. I was in a rut before we all came down to Mexico. I was working like a bastard for *Time*. I was worn out."

"We both were. And look at us now. Here we are right back doing the same damn crap we wanted to get away from," I said.

"It won't last long. Before you know it, we'll be back on the boat bringing in dinner for the six of us," Owen declared.

"Won't that be grand," I said.

"Won't it! I'm damn ready to wrap this ordeal up and get back to San Rafael," Owen said. He leaned back on the hard wooden bench. "Have you ever had a funny feeling, you know that strange queasy feeling that you might have made a bad decision…a stupid decision let's just call it?"

"All my life."

"Well…I wonder—"

"It'll be okay, old boy, you'll see."

"Want to hear something?"

"I'm sure you'll tell me no matter what."

"Well, you know I said that when I was working for *Time*, I never thought about Anna. Said she was just someone from out of my past. Well, that was total bullshit. Total. I thought about her every day. Had these crazy dreams about her all the time. Thought we'd eventually get back together. Why is it that, when it comes to some people, people we can't let go of? Why is that? And then others, they come into our life and then they're gone, and that's it. You know what I'm talking about, Jack. How life grabs onto us at times tight as the talons of an eagle. Why is that?" Owen hunched over and stared at the concrete floor beneath us.

"Wish I knew. You know I'm a pretty crappy shrink."

"Aw…maybe just rethinking a few things, that's all" Owen said.

"It's all right. Everything will be fine, buddy. You'll see," I said. "We'll be back on the boat baiting up our lines with smelly bonita and bringing in snapper and tuna and grouper in no time."

Owen thought for a second and said, "You're probably right. I feel better already."

"And anyway, I need a break from the book."

"Having trouble?"

"Writing isn't easy. And sometimes it isn't fun."

"Too late to be a railroad engineer," Owen said.

"Now that's a good profession. I should give it a try."

"No matter what happens, you'll never abandon the writing and I'll never abandon the camera. We're damn stuck…let's face it. See what we got ourselves into."

"Thought we came to Mexico to live as

expats," I said.

"Oh…did we?"

"Sit in bars and talk to the other expats and find solutions to the world's problems."

"How nice that would be. When can we start?" Owen asked.

"Soon as we get back, I say."

"And give up writing and photography"

"Hell, yes. Why not," I said.

"We'll go to Pablo's or Manny's and drink rum all afternoon and all night like the other expats do."

"Won't that be keen," I said. "By the way, have they solved any problems yet?"

"Sure."

"Like what?" I said.

"Like not punching a clock to make a living."

"You'd make a damn good philosopher, old boy. And a damn good expat, too," I said.

"Then we'll fit in well with the crowd at Pablo's and Manny's."

"After all, we already know how to drink

rum. We've flattened the expat curve a helluva lot," I said.

"And we're pretty good at philosophy, right?" Owen said.

"So, we've got that one figured out, too," I said.

"Shit, we'll be regulars there in no time, you watch."

"Hell, we're already pretty damn good expats. Don't you think? And so are Anna and Chloe."

"And Sophie told me all the parents of the kids she goes to school with are very smart. She said they talk about a lot of very "pacific" stuff. That's what she said. Lots of "pacific" stuff. I believe she means specific. She's still working on her words a bit," Owen said.

"And doing a damn good job, I think."

"Me, I think I'll need a little more time with the rum part of the expat thing. Pretty good with beer and wine but weak with my rum. Never had much till now. What say we do is we all go to one of the cantinas in San Rafael and work on the rum thing—you, me, Anna, Chloe. Anna can get Isabel to sit with the kids. What do you say?" Owen said.

"If it makes us better expats, hell yes," I replied.

"And I'll grow a big beard and pretend I'm Hemingway drinking rum at La Floridita, the gin mill in Cuba he used to go to where he put away all those daquiris with Castro and the others."

"He had the expat thing figured out pretty damn well, didn't he? Paris, Key West, Bimini, Cuba. The only place he missed was San Rafael," I said.

After what seemed like an hour but was probably no more than twenty minutes, voices came from the room where the man had been working on the tire. A very serious discussion of some type.

"Okay, they're going to take us to Martinez," Owen said quietly.

Soon, the man came into the back room and told us to come with him. We walked down to the Land Rover and gathered Owen's cameras and my laptop.

The man nodded for us to follow. A vehicle had pulled up by the garage. A man got out and opened the back door and we climbed in. The driver leaned over and told us to fasten our seatbelts, the ride would be rough. He handed us blindfolds and told us to put them on. It was necessary if we wanted to go meet Martinez.

The vehicle started down the road, hard and rough. It was unnerving sitting in the back not able to see. I felt as though we were being led to the gallows, but I pushed the thought from my mind. The driver was alone. The ride was quiet but for an occasional stone from the dirt road that snapped up onto the bottom of the car. We knew not to talk.

Several times the car slowed, giving the impression it was about to stop, but it kept onward. It was easy to tell that we were going up and down hills, just as when we rode to the small village of San Christi. Even with the mask I could smell the lush green vegetation and the mountain air outside the car. It made me think of how blind people can see with their nose and ears in ways that the rest of us have forfeited most of our senses to only what we can see.

We turned off the road, if that's what it was, and began moving at what seemed like not more than ten miles an hour. Plants swept along the side of the vehicle and branches and twigs cracked under the wheels. We slowed to a stop.

The driver got out and talked to a man. I understood some of what they said. He mentioned that we were the two gringos from a magazine that wanted a story. Soon, the driver opened the backdoor, and said we could get out, and told us we could take off our masks.

We were in a small camp, that was obvious immediately. It consisted of a few tents, some cooking equipment, and one rifle leaning against a tent.

A man came over. He wore brown cargo pants and a Baltimore Orioles baseball cap. He had deep piercing eyes, and a stubbly mustache. A mutt stood dutifully at his side.

He shook our hands in a way that spoke of

sincerity.

"Jack Carter," I said. "This is Owen Brookes."

"Javier Martinez, and this fellow here is George. I'm told you are from *Time* magazine," Martinez said in English that was clear and good, as though he had spent time outside of Mexico at some point.

I rubbed George's ears, causing his eyes to close in satisfaction.

"Yes, and we'd like to do a story about your work," Owen said.

"We can go inside." Martinez led us into a large tent that had three canvas chairs as if he was expecting us. We took a chair. George spread out on the ground next to Martinez.

"Bring a bottle, if you would be so kind," Martinez said to one of his companions.

Soon the man entered with tequila and three small glasses. Martinez filled them and handed one to each of us. He sat in a chair and leaned back and breathed in the fragrance of the tart amber liquor and, without taking any, set the glass on a small table.

"May I record?" I asked.

"Yes. But nothing about our location here…in the event it got out."

"No, nothing. Anyway, I'm not exactly sure where we are."

"So, well…you may not know it, but I am the one who got your boss Bauer to do the story," Martinez said. "I met him some time ago. We got along very well. But I understand that like all journalists, like all magazines, what he really wants is a story. That's okay. Information about our cause is what's important. We want it to be told." He took a sip of the tequila. "I'll give you some background. We might as well start at the beginning, I suppose. Yes, I am Javier Martinez. I come from a wealthy and influential family in the old provincial city of San Luis Potosi deep in the central desert. My father was a prominent lawyer there. I had a good education, first thinking I would be a lawyer like him, then I decided my best contribution to mankind would be as a medical doctor."

"And, so, when was that?" I asked.

"When was that? Let's see. When I was about twenty, I guess. That was my goal in life—to make a positive contribution to the world. I was taught this from my father and mother. They had learned it from their parents and grandparents. There is a long history of such in my family. I was very lucky and was able to go to a good medical school up in the States. In Texas, in fact, at the Health Science Center in Houston. It is a massive complex and you can get the best training in the world there. I was unsure what I wanted to be…the kind of doctor, I mean. But eventually I did additional training in internal medicine."

"In Houston also?"

"No. I got lucky and did a residency at the Johns Hopkins Hospital in Baltimore." He aimed his thumb at his Orioles baseball cap, smiled, and said, "Yes, at Hopkins in Baltimore and sometimes sitting in a crab house with all my buddies from school, all my *compadres*, eating crabs and drinking National Bohemian beer…Natty Boh, they call it," he added with a hardy laugh.

"Almost as good as the stuff down here."

"We know about the good Mexican beers," Owen said.

Martinez nodded. "Bauer told me you are both living in Mexico. Is that right?"

"Over in the Yucatan…a small town called San Rafael on the Caribbean."

Martinez leaned back and held the glass to his lips and took a small sip. "And what brought you to Mexico?"

"We are trying to leave the world," Owen said in a solid yet jocular way.

"Hmm…is that possible?" Martinez asked.

"The jury is quite out," I replied.

"I'm afraid, my friends, the world…well…it knows we are all here," Martinez said. "It will not let us just slip away. Not so easily, at least."

"I think you're right," Owen grimly replied. "But we are trying, nonetheless."

"Yes, I too even I wish I could do that sometimes. But I know I can't," Martinez said, glancing away for a second. "So anyway, when I came back from the states, I began practicing here in Mexico. First, I joined a small clinic in a town in the state of Zacatecas, a very poor state in the center of the mining industry…lead and copper and some silver and gold, that stuff. The people overall are poor and not well educated. I spent seven years there, but it is difficult to take care of people when they need so much more than treatment for ten minutes."

Martinez went on to explain that everyone in his family had been raised to have a concern for social justice, and that his father was a well-known lawyer who had a good practice and also took on many pro bono cases. "He was the Atticus Finch of San Luis Potosi. Remember Atticus Finch? *To Kill a Mockingbird.* He was a good man. My father, also. He wanted to help everyone, but he knew he couldn't, and it bothered him. He passed away a few years ago. I think he worked himself to death, worried himself to death, at least. We all miss him."

"A big change to what you are doing now," Owen said.

"The government likes to call us revolutionaries," Martinez said with an uneasy frown. "But we're not…not in the classic version of that. Our tactics are not those of guerilla fighters. For one thing, we have people in every part of the State of Chiapas, not just up in these little mountain camps, but all throughout the state. Our goal is to change the thinking of the people, the peasants. Consider this, the government knows that to control the peasants, you must first control how they think. It is a psychological war we are in. All throughout the hills you will see signs telling the peasants that we are trying to take their land away from them."

"Yes, we saw many of the signs along the road all throughout Chiapas. They paint you in very bad light," I said.

"We are aware. We know the government is working on the minds of the people." Martinez tapped the side of his head.

"And you?"

"Mexico fought a bloody revolution from 1910 all the way to about 1917. At that time the government of Porfirio Diaz was defeated and Venustiano Carranza became president. A new constitution was drawn up. Since then, Mexico has swung back and forth through good leaders to corrupt ones. Very little of the land reform and the rights of the people that were promised at the end of the revolution ever came about despite the lofty rhetoric you hear from the politicians at election times."

"Your task seems formidable," I said.

"But I have no plans or desire to be a politician. Nothing would please me more than to go back to practicing medicine in a rural clinic."

Martinez finished his tequila and refilled the glasses all around. I saw a weary look in his face. Eyes that drooped for a man of his young age. It was easy to predict that the task he had undertaken had taken a considerable toll on him.

"How long will you continue your effort," I asked.

"When a person has been told they have cancer, they become very determined. Their whole life takes on purpose that it never had before. I know as a doctor that you never ask a cancer patient how long do you want to fight to live? They will say, 'As long as I can'. Sometimes, occasionally, a person will realize the battle is lost and they want to go out peacefully. But that is different. What we are doing now is not something I can just walk away from."

Light from an old lamp with a trimmed wick filled the tent with flickering, tawdry light.

Owen took two cameras from his bag. One with a 28mm lens and one with a 35mm lens. He snapped off a half dozen shots with each camera, then rested the cameras on his lap, ready raise one to his eye and again capture the ever-determined expressions that Martinez' face revealed. Martinez talked as if Owen were not present.

"And, anyway, it would be very hard to mount a military offensive even if we wanted to. They know almost every move we make. It's not like the old days. The government has sophisticated ways to track us. Satellite images. Drones. I am quite sure they followed your trip here almost from when you left Billie Carrigan's place.

That is why our only hope is to win over the hearts of the people."

"Are you making progress?" I asked.

Martinez shrugged. "Some. But it is not easy. You would think it would be. You would think people who have so little would want to change in ways that help them. But when you have almost nothing," he pinched his fingers together, "yes, when that's all you have, your biggest worry is that you will lose even that. That you will lose everything. And then you end up with nothing. It is easier to cling onto what you have, as small as it might be, than to lose it all."

"And how many people do you have working with you?"

"Oh, several hundred, I guess…in one form or another. You already met several. Our fight, if you will, has many soldiers each doing a job. It is truly like in any army where you have people with many different duties. Some people are good at working with the peasants. Others just help in little ways. This is what makes us strong. It would be very difficult for the government to find everyone in our dedicated army. And even if they did, what would they do? Haul us all in and throw us all in jail? They know they can't do that. It would cause a crisis that the world would notice. This is why it is important that you are here today. For the world to see and maybe learn. Maybe when people pick up a copy of *Time* magazine at the supermarket and take it home and read about this, they will understand what we are trying to do. Maybe." Martinez reached down and scratched George's head. "You can meet the people, the ones we are trying to reach…the locals, the villagers."

# 4

Morning brought the call of a rooster from a farm somewhere down the road. Though I slept well, I awoke feeling stiff and in need of coffee. Owen and Martinez were already up, sitting in the shade of a ceiba tree that spread high over the tents.

"Up here on top of the green hills of the Chiapas mountains, it is hard to believe anything in the world could be wrong," I said.

Martinez nodded, as if he himself had felt that way many times. "Amigo," he said, pointing to the coffee pot and a cup. "Please, have some. Ah, see how beautiful it is here," he said. "I think there is no place on earth as nice as this. Hear the silence? Oh my, how beautiful it is. Even for people who have nothing." He waved a hand generously, as if referring to all who lived in the hills around us, "Even those people, they too, have this. No matter what, nobody can take away the beauty God has given them. That's what they believe."

"It is easy to understand, isn't it?" I said.

"When you come down to it, people don't want a lot out of life," Martinez said. "People are the same the world over. That I believe. You see when I worked in the clinics in the poor towns in Zacatecas, I realized that it was not different from when I was a medical resident working with the people living in Highlandtown in Baltimore. Or the people out in east Baltimore, in Essex or Dundalk. Everyone's needs are the same. Everyone's aspirations and hopes are the same."

One of Martinez' companions set a stack of sweet breads before us. "Please, amigos, take one. They are from the village nearby. I am sure you will love them. Me, I can't start my day without one," he said, then added, "Or maybe *two*." He laughed a laugh I was becoming familiar with.

As we ate sweetbread and drank coffee, Martinez said. "We will go down to one of the very small villages where we are working with the people, the peasants. I don't bring a gun to one of these places. Seeing it worries the people and they begin to believe the propaganda the government is dishing out. They believe we are planning to take their land and make them work on a coffee plantation up in the hills somewhere. And anyway, I've never had to use a gun and I doubt that I will need to now."

"Can I photograph?" Owen said. "It will be important for the article."

Martinez nodded. "It will be all right. I will explain it to them if necessary."

"So, does the government knows about us being here? What do you think?"

"Hah…the government knows everything. They should spend more time taking care of the needs of the people than worrying about us. They will know who you are and that you are from a magazine, and they will not like that, but there is little they can do. You can think of yourselves as a sort of insurance policy for us today," Martinez said, cracking a smile.

After we had coffee and breakfast, Martinez loaded the Jeep and we left camp. Martinez drove—another man next to him up front, Owen and I in the back. The sun was angling up over the mountain top. Martinez took the road at barely twenty miles an hour, now and then speaking over his shoulder in a nonchalant way as if merely on a Sunday afternoon road trip.

We came down one hill after another. If we had been at eight thousand feet, I estimated we descended to four thousand or so. The air was different—closer, warmer. The villages were as simple and plain as a worn-out penny. It was easy to grasp the fullness of the lives in the villages and the small houses.

Riding along, I said to Martinez, "It occurs to me that you are a lot like Che Guevara. You are a doctor just as he was and, like him, you want to make life better for the people."

"I do not think of myself as being much like

Che. Yes, he was a doctor also. And he often treated people with little compensation for his work. I have done that as well. But as I mentioned before, I am not a revolutionary, not the way he was. By no means am I a guerilla trying to take over the government. If anything, I am like Che's best friend…."

"Camilo Cinfuegos," Owen said quickly.

"Indeed, Camilo Cinfuegos," Martinez replied. "I am surprised you know of him."

"I only know he was a good friend of Che's," Owen said.

"And a very happy man, they say. He loved people. He is my model more than anyone, I suppose."

"And from what I know, a good model to have," Owen said.

"Yes…yes, he loved to laugh and to make jokes and to make others laugh. There is a certain gift in being able to do that. I cannot do it the way he did. And he loved his cigars. All the Cuban fighters did, of course. Me, I don't smoke cigars. They aren't good for your health and, anyway, they make my stomach grouchy and very unhappy." He patted his tummy and laughed. "But it is good that they do that because then I am not tempted to smoke them."

At mid-morning we pulled into the small village of Santiago El Pinar.

"This is it," Martinez declared, stopping the car in town near the zocalo. "We have worked here quite a bit in the past. We might be making some progress…I don't know…might."

We hadn't been there long when a man came up to us. He was introduced by Martinez as the mayor of the small hamlet.

"This is Hernando Gutierrez," Martinez told us. "A wonderful, hardworking man who runs this great place."

Hernando Gutierrez broke into a smile that brought out every line in his round dark face.

"I see you have two *compadres*," Gutierrez said.

"Yes. From a magazine. *Time*."

"We have an election coming up soon in the state of Chiapas," Gutierrez said. "It's a very important election. One of the candidates is a man from our group. A very good man who wants to make sure the people get what they deserve, just like Doctor Javier here. Our candidate wants to see to it that all the people get good medical attention."

"Yes," Martinez said. "The government is supposed to provide it for the people, but the system is a mess and needs to be fixed from top to bottom. Because of that, poor people don't go to a doctor. It is too much trouble, and they cannot afford to miss work."

"We will be printing up signs for our candidate and placing them all around the area. The goal is to outdo what the government does in its campaign, "Gutierrez said. "That is not easy to do, however." He held his hand up to the sky. "But I believe God is on our side."

"And what about the church? They should be able to help your cause...am I correct?" I asked.

Martinez shook his head. "It depends. Some of the priests are with us. But some are not. The older priests especially—the ones that the elderly people in the village respect the most because they have listened to their sermons for most of their lives. *And,* you may not think it, but those are the people who always vote. The priest might say do not vote for one of the candidates that we are supporting because they are all communists and they want to take your land and make you work on state-owned farms. Unfortunately, many of his flock believe it."

"That is very true," Gutierrez said. "But we have a good priest here in Santiago. A young priest who understands and supports us and our cause. The people in this village, most of them, listen carefully to what he says. But it is not like that everywhere. When we campaign in other villages, it is an uphill battle sometimes." He shook his head and raised his hands in disbelief. "So…come with me and I'll show you what we are doing."

We followed Gutierrez to the other side of the zocalo and a half block down a cobblestone street to an office where inside three people, a man and two women, were working.

"Here, we are putting together campaign signs for our candidates," Gutierrez said. "You can see the name of our party: People's Democratic Party...the PDP. Many people in other countries are not aware that Mexico is a democracy, just like the US. We have a Senate and a Chamber of Deputies, as it is called, which is very much like your House of Representatives. The PDP is considered a splinter group, but we have candidates in almost every state. Even if we did not have enough members elected to control the Senate or the Chamber, we still could make a difference when it comes to changing laws. That is how we see it and it is our goal."

We spent more time talking to other members of the PDP.

A priest came into the office and was introduced to us. He was very young, with soft brown eyes and a kind face. He talked about his support for reform.

"I must be careful what I say, however," the priest said. "It is inappropriate for me to discuss political matters in the pulpit. But the people know who I support, and I think it makes a difference in their thinking. I am like Martinez and Gutierrez here. I only want what is best for the people. For many years the Catholic church has had a deep fear of communism, especially here in Latin America. It is easy for the leaders of the church, the bishops and the cardinals, to believe that political change will result in a communist overtake of the government."

The bells of the Angelus rang at the noon hour; the priest and Gutierrez and Martinez and the others in the room knelt with their heads down and hands folded as the priest recited the Angelus while the bells tolled.

When they arose, the priest smiled and luminously said, "Come…come, let's have a good lunch. What do you say? We will go over to Juanita's restaurant. What do you say?"

I was famished. The ride had been long and bumpy, a good lunch was welcomed at this point.

Juanita's was a clean and cheerful place with good windows that let in much light.

Gutierrez led us to a table.

"What a lucky day," Juanita said, as she approached. "All my favorite people. And who are these you have brought with you?"

Gutierrez explained who we were and talked about the article we would be doing.

"Then you have selected the best people to lead you," Juanita said. "Doctor. Javier comes to our village frequently to talk with Señor Gutierrez. And, of course, we all know and love our dear priest." She put her hands together and bowed her head.

"And, at no place on all of the earth is there a better cantina than Juanita's," the priest replied.

"Uh, he is always so kind. Well, what will it be today for lunch?" Juanita said.

Later in the day, Martinez took us to two small villages. Gutierrez joined us. At each place, they talked to the villagers and told them a very important election was soon coming up and it was important that as many people as possible voted. I watched the villagers. You could tell that many of them were wary of getting involved.

Martinez asked if he could leave a few signs with the names of the candidates. They usually agreed but told him it was a waste of time; the government comes by almost immediately and rips them out. In every village, the story was the same.

Owen captured a few frames of Martinez and Gutierrez talking to the people.

# 5

That evening we sat by the tents and ate charro beans that one of Martinez men had prepared. George chewed a meat bone, gnawing patiently with a set of large molars.

Martinez talked in his usual calm and introspective way. I sensed that he wanted to apologize for what he perceived had been a sad failure in demonstrating success with the movement, fearing perhaps that this might be the final take-home message from the day and that we might paint a picture that Martinez' work was futile.

After a brief silence, hunched over dinner, Martinez spoke quietly saying, "Well…you can see where we are. The government has scared the hell out of them. The peasants have two strikes against them. They are poor and they are unedu-cated." He stopped talking and slowly stirred the cup of beans and looked away. Turning again to us, he softly said, "Well, I still believe we can succeed."

"What will it take?" Owen asked.

"On our part, much persistence. The govern-ment wants us to give up. But you cannot do that. Remember what I said about a patient fighting a very bad disease? This is no different. It is im-portant not to quit."

"And you truly believe in your heart you will win?" I felt compelled to ask.

"Yes, absolutely, I *know* we can. I know we will. Much like I said yesterday, we are not trying to overthrow the government. We are trying to fix it from within. Our successes come in small amounts. One candidate…maybe just one…gets elected. And then pretty soon we have a few more in the government who understand the people, who *truly* understand the people. We build it that way. That is our goal."

Martinez poured tequila for each of us. He

looked like a man in need of it. "*Salud!*" he said.

"So, how are your charro beans?" he asked.

"*Magnifico*," I replied.

This made Martinez smile. "Yes, Miguel is our master chef here."

"He is good. You must let him know," Owen stated.

"I always do."

"What's in store for tomorrow?" I asked.

"Another village I want you to see. It is one we have made good progress with. It is a bit bigger than Santiago and many of the people are receptive to us. Many of the younger people especially want to hear what we have to say. The older people resist, but even with some of them we are making progress."

"This will be good for the article," Owen said.

"I should tell you, though. It is an area where we have had trouble with the military. More so than any other place. The government is concerned about how we are chipping away at the progress they are making."

Owen pulled up his shirt and showed Martinez where a bullet had ripped through his lower abdomen.

Martinez threw his head back and laughed. "And it looks like it sidestepped your liver and the ascending colon," he said, laughing more. "You have been very lucky, my friend. Well, so far anyway, we have all been okay. Tomorrow should be no different. They like to shower us with a rain of bullets from time to time. See, they are little boys. They think by pretending they are tough that we will quit and give up. It is not that simple. You just do not do that."

"The town is called San Marcos, a dozen or so miles across the valley from where we were today. It is a larger community—harder for the government to gain control of the minds of the people. If you feel safe going there, we can talk to the people. We have a good organization there and a very good candidate for local office whose name is Antonio Aguilar. He is running for a position as a state Senator here in Chiapas."

"And what would you say his chances are?"

"Very good, from what we can tell so far."

"I think this will be a good addition to the article," I said.

*

That night I had a dark and morbid dream. The same dream I had come to know most of my life. I was a young child sleeping in bed. I heard someone at the doorway and looked over. My father, Big Hank, stood there talking slowly and calmy as if not to startle me.

"It's me, Jack," he said. I just want to…just wanted to…well…well, to…you need to be very careful. If you are not careful, you can get hurt. I wish I could be with you, but I cannot. I should be with you, I know it. If I were with you, I would see that everything is fine. But I will be going now. I don't even wonder why that is. I cannot answer it myself. It is just who I am, I guess…I guess."

He stopped talking. I wanted to reach out to him. I wanted him to come over and hug me, come over and give me a kiss. But he did not. He said, "I love you, Jack." Then turned and closed the door.

The dream changed and I saw the face of the man. The face of Big Hank, my father, more clearly than ever before. And I saw tears on his face. And then, as he did in every dream, he said, "I'm sorry, Jack," and left.

# 6

In the morning I arose tired and headachy. I had a vivid memory of the dream that seemed somehow dolefully prescient. I tried to push it from my mind.

I had coffee and sweet bread with the others and then we climbed into the Jeep. This time one of Martinez' men drove; Martinez was next to him up front.

Looking at the sky, Martinez again commented on the beauty of mornings up in the hills of Chiapas. He loved the soft, serene breezes that filled the air. The scents of food coming from the kitchens of the houses as we passed through small hamlets.

"Another thirty minutes probably and we'll be there." Martinez said, in a buoyant voice.

He had barely finished the sentence when a blast of bullets came over our heads.

"Down!" Martinez yelled. "The boys are at it just like I said they would be." He signaled to the driver to speed up.

After a several dozen rounds, the spray of bullets ended. The driver angled the Jeep down the road, seemingly hitting every rut and pothole and groove the road offered.

"How the hell did they know we were coming here today?" I called to Martinez.

"They know everything we do. I don't know how," Martinez said.

"Well, they are damn good at it," Owen said.

"Yes, everywhere we go." Martinez sat up slightly. "We are probably okay now. The little boys are just playing one of their games."

"A deadly serious one, it seems," I said.

"So far, only a game."

"Bullets flying around you are not so easy to get used to. This I know," Owen said.

"And not at all good for one's blood pressure," Martinez said, tapping his hand over his heart.

Twenty minutes later, we pulled into the village.

Martinez turned to the back seat. "So, are my companions okay? See what poor shots they are…we are all fine," he said.

"Plenty close enough," I said.

Martinez laughed heavy and hard.

"It only matters when it is too close," Owen offered.

"So now…shall we continue?" Martinez asked, making sure we wanted to go on with the visit as planned.

"*Vamanos*," Owen said.

We climbed from the Jeep. A young man roughly Martinez' age came out of a building. Martinez introduced us.

"It is very good that you are here today, Doctor Javier," the man said. "You see, Señor Aguilar will be talking to the people about what he wants to do when he is in the Senate. He is over in the community hall now. Come, let's go over. Let's meet him."

We went to a simple room in which rows of chairs had been set up. People were coming in and taking seats. Martinez took us to meet Aguilar. He smiled kindly and shook our hands like any good politician would, as if we, ourselves, would be casting a vote in the election.

When the room was nearly full, Aguilar took the microphone and began addressing the group in a peaceful and sincere voice. He explained in simple terms his goals and the goals of the PDP, and why the government candidates had no intentions of helping the people despite what they say.

Owen captured a series of images as Aguilar walked slowly across the front of the room and talked to the people. After an hour, Aguilar thanked everyone for coming and encouraged them to vote. People of all ages, more than I expected, stayed and shook Aguilar's hand and said they were grateful for what he would do if elected.

We remained until the afternoon, meeting people from the PDP. This time, I felt as though we managed to get a true portrayal of what Martinez and his group were attempting to do.

The sun had begun to turn to the west, bringing with it crisp, cool air. We climbed into Martinez Jeep. I could tell he was in good spirits and that he felt good about the progress they were making in the village. He thought the PDP might do well in the election and he liked the way Aguilar related to the people and how they seemed to believe him.

We hadn't gone far, ten miles, maybe more, it was hard to be certain on the rough road. I sat in the back making notes; Owen flipped through the images from the day. Suddenly, a torrent of bullets flew past us once again. We immediately ducked into the Jeep. The driver's nose barely above the steering wheel.

From our morning encounter, I felt as though this would be no more than intimidation by the little boys, as Martinez called them.

Then everything changed. In an instant, a bullet tore through the left front tire. The Jeep tilted to the left.

"Keep going!" Martinez said.

The driver leaned out and looked at the tire. "She still has some air. We might be all right."

We bumbled our way farther down the road, but the ruts and potholes and the soft front tire made for slow travel.

"You're doing good," Martinez said. "Keep going. If we can get up the road a ways, we might be able to change the tire…or, if necessary, I can call the camp and have someone get us."

I looked at Owen, who had a camera poised for action.

Martinez sat up slightly. "We might be all right now. This I can tell you, however. The hole in the tire was not caused by a stray bullet. Those little bastards knew what they were doing." He turned to us. "Everyone okay back there?"

"Yes," Owen and I said in unison.

"Good. Well…the little boys seem to be getting more determined."

"And better shots, too," I said.

"Another mile and we can change the tire. Or maybe swing over and pick up a larger road.

It's a little out of the way but at least they won't bother us there."

Owen put a 35mm wide-angle lens onto his camera and snapped off a series of shots of Martinez and the driver, then leaned out the side of the Jeep and captured a dozen more of the tire. "It's thumping a lot," he said, pulling back onto his seat. "Probably still losing air."

The driver held tight onto the wheel, fighting the back-and-forth wobble created by the tire.

"They knew we were coming this way," Martinez said. "They probably had someone in the group where Aguilar was speaking. They do that almost everywhere we go. Someone's always in the audience listening. They are good at masquerading as villagers. They know the route we will be following when we leave…it's how they set up their ambushes."

"I think it's now losing much air," The driver said.

"A little farther and we will stop and change it. I know this road very well. There is a good place up ahead to do that," Martinez said.

Less than a mile down the road, Martinez said, "Okay, here, this is it. Pull over here."

The road was empty but for us. The driver stopped. We climbed out. Martinez looked quickly around. An uncomfortable expression spread across his face.

Owen took the chance to photograph the tire that was now all but flat.

Martinez unbolted the spare from the back of the Jeep while the driver hurried to place a jack under the left side. All went well. Working fast, the driver had the old tire off and was tightening the lugs on the new one.

"That's it," Martinez said. "Let's get the hell out of here…huh?"

Before we could climb in the Jeep, we found ourselves again surrounded by a blast of gunfire. We flattened on the ground. Bullets tore into the side of the Jeep just inches above us. This was far different from anything so far—closer, more deadly. Yet, they could have easily left us all on the ground in a lake of blood. Why did they not?

We were easy targets.

"Stay down, don't move," Martinez said. "There is little we can do now. For the moment, we are stuck."

I could see that Owen desperately wanted to capture the episode on film. He turned on his side and fidgeted with his camera and held it above him and blindly snapped off a string of images of the Jeep and of us on the ground. He was pushing the envelope, to my way of thinking. But that was Owen.

Instantly, the gunfire ceased.

"Wait a little longer," Martinez said. "When we are sure it is over, we will leave quickly. Once we are down the road a ways, we should be fine."

Three minutes went by. Four minutes. A little longer.

"Okay. Now! Lets' go!" Martinez said. *"Quick! Quick!"*

Almost to the second, as we were climbing in the Jeep, I heard a single gunshot. It sounded like little more than a firecracker. I turned and saw Martinez grab his chest. He rested a hand on the Jeep for support, then fell face down on the ground. A bullet hole in the back of his shirt in his upper chest.

I raced over and turned him on his back. A stream of blood gushed from above his clavicle.

Owen ripped off his shirt and pressed it tightly onto the wound.

Blood continued to spew out. Owen continued to press on the wound.

I looked at Martinez. His eyes turned to me. He attempted to speak. His mouth quivered. At that second the pupils of his eyes became wide and black and fixed.

Owen put two fingers on Martinez' neck, searching for a pulse. "Oh, my God, no," he said. He lowered his head and breathed a long breath and quietly said, "He's gone…he's gone."

# Part 3

# 1

Three weeks later, our article appeared in *Time* with a photo of Martinez on the cover and many more images of him in the magazine. They reminded me of the gentle and dedicated man we had met in Chiapas. I had made an effort to accurately portray the soft-spoken man-of-the-people without giving him supernatural qualities. It was a difficult task, but when I read the article, I felt good about my description of him and of his aspirations. At least we had a chance to tell the world about this man and the causes that motivated him so ardently.

Upon returning from Chiapas, we told Chloe and Anna what had happened, how a simple trip to write a simple article had turned so sourly tragic right before our eyes. Such events were not unknown to Owen during his days working in the Middle East. For me, they only existed in fiction. Both Owen and I vowed it would be the last story we would do.

Life in San Rafael gradually returned for us. But when life deals a sudden and chilling blow, it takes time to recover, assuming it is even possible.

We spent most days on the water. I worked on my book, though progress was slower than ever. Owen quietly printed a mountain of work he had accumulated over the years that would become part of a book from his photojournalism days. Chloe continued to paint—work that always got better and better. And Anna, of course, spent her time with Danny and Sophie.

I sat at my desk staring at the computer screen. Was there any chance I would be able to finish my book now? My life seemed to have turned inside out. How to overcome the tragedy we had experienced? What does the world do when a man like Martinez is taken from it? Is there true justice in life on this planet? Or is it a mirage that we all use to move us onward to the next day—that and nothing more? Another day believing life has meaning. Believing life is good. I had no answer and the more I thought about it, the more I realized my book was a failure, and I had yet to finish it. I was trying to write about the American dream. But now I believed that at times all dreams are a hoax—a big goddam hoax. And I knew that we merely cling to these dreams out of inherent desperation.

"Hi, Mr. Jack," The voice behind me said.

"Hi, Sophie," I said, turning. "You haven't been around in a while."

"My mother said not to bother you. She hopes you are working on your book."

I smiled and nodded.

"She told me not to mention the book. She knew I would."

"It's not a problem," I humbly uttered.

"Do you need a new window to look out of? Maybe that will help."

"That's a good idea, but I will be fine here, I think."

"My mother says I have ESP. I don't know what that is, but she tells me it pisses her off. That's what she says."

"Well, ESP is when we can tell what other people are thinking. She might be right…about you and ESP, I think."

"Is it bad to have ESP?"

"No, there is no harm in it."

"Will they take me to the doctor and have me checked out some way. I don't like going to the doctor."

"I'm sure they won't. I think you will be fine."

"Except that it pisses my mother off."

I laughed. "Your mother will be fine, too. I think she was kidding around with you."

"Do you think so?"

"Sure."

"Were you thinking about moving to a new window to look out of?"

"Oh…I might have thought of it. See, you do have ESP."

"If you move to a different window, maybe

you can write real fast."

"You know, I never thought of it like that."

"Is it good to write real fast…and finish the book real fast?"

"Some people think so."

"Well, I think it's a good idea."

"Then I would have to start writing something else again."

"Or you could just go fishing with Owen every day and not have to write at all. Are you going to go fishing?"

"Pretty soon probably."

"Today?"

"Oh…possibly."

"If you don't, what will we have for dinner?"

"How about tacos. We could all go down to Ricardo's Restaurant in San Rafael and have tacos. How does that sound?"

"Do you think we can? I like tacos almost as much as I like fish. Do you like going to San Rafael?" Sophie asked.

"Oh, yeah. It's a swell place."

"My mother said there are a lot of expats who go to the bars to drink big margaritas and things in San Rafael. She said I probably go to school with their kids. What is an expat?"

"Well, people like us, I guess. Like me and Owen and Chloe and your mother. People who left their country to live someplace else."

"Why would people do that?"

"That's a good question. I haven't quite figured it out yet."

Sophie smiled as if she had come up with the answer. "Did you do it so you don't have to work too hard and can go fishing in the sea every day?"

"You must be reading my mind again. See how great your ESP is."

"What did you do when you and Owen went on your trip to Chiapas? I know where Chiapas is. We studied it in school."

I breathed in slowly. "We wrote a story for a magazine."

"Was it a good story?"

"Someday I'll tell you."

"—kay. I have to go now. Bye, Mr. Jack."

"Bye Sophie."

As she was leaving, she turned and said, "Let's have tacos for dinner tonight. Do you think we can?"

"I'm sure we can."

"Cool!"

I looked out the window. No, I would not sit in front of a different window. I knew that had nothing to do with my malaise. The sea was the sea, and the sky was the sky, and my writing was my writing. I thought about our attempt at living as expats. It seemed like a foolish endeavor, just like it probably was for all the others who drank big margaritas in San Rafael.